新英文選

（上）

黃正興　編著

Studies serve for delight, for ornament, and for ability.~Francis Bacon

三民書局

網路書店位址　http://www.sanmin.com.tw

© 新 英 文 選 (上)

編著者	黃正興
發行人	劉振強
著作財產權人	三民書局股份有限公司 臺北市復興北路386號
發行所	三民書局股份有限公司 地址／臺北市復興北路386號 電話／(02)25006600 郵撥／0009998-5
印刷所	三民書局股份有限公司
門市部	復北店／臺北市復興北路386號 重南店／臺北市重慶南路一段61號
初版一刷	中華民國八十九年八月
初版四刷	中華民國九十二年十月

編　號　S 803030

行政院新聞局登記證局版臺業字第○二○○號

KK音標發音符號表

母音	例	子音	例
[i]	eat [it]; sheep [ʃip]	[p]	park [pɑrk]; soup [sup]
[ɪ]	it [ɪt]; kick [kɪk]	[b]	but [bʌt]; Bob [bɑb]
[e]	make [mek]; day [de]	[t]	too [tu]; tent [tɛnt]
[ɛ]	pen [pɛn]; end [ɛnd]	[d]	do [du]; stand [stænd]
[æ]	pan [pæn]; bad [bæd]	[k]	seek [sik]; car [kɑr]
[ɑ]	box [bɑks]; not [nɑt]	[g]	good [gud]; dog [dɔg]
[ɔ]	dog [dɔg]; caught [kɔt]	[f]	foot [fut];laugh [læf]
[o]	note [not]; flow [flo]	[v]	very [ˈvɛrɪ]; of [əv]
[ʊ]	book [bʊk]; cook [kʊk]	[θ]	three [θri]; mouth [maʊθ]
[u]	cool [kul]; lose [luz]	[ð]	that [ðæt]; father [ˈfɑðɚ]
[ɝ]	nurse [nɝs]; earn [ɝn]	[s]	so [so]; ask [æsk]
[ɚ]	teacher [ˈtitʃɚ]; better [ˈbɛtɚ]	[z]	zoo [zu]; yours [jurz]
[ə]	America [əˈmɛrɪkə]; of [əv]	[ʃ]	she [ʃi]; wash [waʃ]
[ʌ]	up [ʌp]; cut [kʌt]	[ʒ]	closure [ˈkloʒɚ]; vision [ˈvɪʒən]
[aɪ]	I [aɪ]; write [raɪt]	[h]	hot [hɑt]; he [hi]
[aʊ]	hour [aʊr]; now [naʊ]	[tʃ]	chair [tʃɛr]; teach [titʃ]
[ɔɪ]	boy [bɔɪ]; voice [vɔɪs]	[dʒ]	joke [dʒok]; page [pedʒ]
		[m]	my [maɪ]; come [kʌm]
		[m̩]	keep'em [ˈkipm̩]
		[n]	no [no]; on [ɑn]
		[n̩]	cotton [ˈkɑtn̩]; season [ˈsizn̩]
		[ŋ]	thank [θæŋk]; sing [sɪŋ]
		[l]	lot [lɑt]; sell [sɛl]
		[l̩]	little [ˈlɪtl̩]; sample [ˈsæmpl̩]
		[w]	we [wi]; wait [wet]
		[hw]	what [hwɑt]; where [hwɛr]
		[j]	yes [jɛs]; yard [jɑrd]
		[r]	run [rʌn]; rock [rɑk]

序　言

　　英國文豪培根 (Francis Bacon, 1561–1626) 於《論讀書》(Of Studies) 中曾說：「讀書能使人獲得樂趣、文飾和能力。」(Studies serve for delight, for ornament, and for ability.) 樂趣來自於生活上之體會，可提供獨處時心靈上的充實，及與人溝通時話題上的交集；文飾來自於藝術人文氣息方面之薰陶，可提供於談話時，表現出讀書的文雅氣息與人文優雅動人的言詞。另外，讀書能提供科學經驗與新知，以瞭解科學萬物之奧秘與邏輯，獲得智慧的能力，以作為處理事物之指針。

　　本書內容即針對此讀書功能目標「樂趣、文飾和能力」而訂，亦構成本書的特色，如下：

1. 充實的課文內容

  (1)增強樂趣：在生活溝通方面有

　　Talking to People

　　Do-It-Yourself

　　Culture Shock

  (2)增強文飾：在藝術人文方面有

　　William Shakespeare

　　Your Personality in the Palm of Your Hand?

  (3)增強能力：在科學自然方面有

　　What Happened to the Dinosaurs?

　　The Day a Mountain Died

　　Controlling the Forest

2. 有趣的小故事

　　趣味小故事 (Short Story) 內容則以趣味為導向，可提供課後休閒閱讀之用，使閱讀文章成為有趣的生活泉源，有利於培養健康有益的閱讀習慣。其主要分類如下：

  (1)人文感人方面

The Flower
A Brother Like That
A Story from Mexico
(2)風俗本土方面
Chinese New Year Customs
Thanksgiving Days
Festivals of New Year
Christmas Traditions
(3)偉人介紹方面
Helen Keller

3. 精鍊的練習與文法

　　每課皆設計有獨到的練習，有是非題、生字、閱讀瞭解測驗、問答、克漏字、片語、配合題、詞類變化、翻譯、文法等。透過有系統的練習，達到精鍊的重複學習效果。

系統的文法整理練習

　　從基本的文法、名詞、代名詞、形容詞、冠詞、副詞、動詞、連接詞、介系詞等，做有系統的整理，並以各類重要考試之考題作為範例講解，理論配合實務，簡明扼要，清晰明瞭，以求「現學現用」之立即學習效果。

培根有言：「知識即是力量。」(Knowledge is power.) 又人常言：「開卷有益。」本文選即在提供有益之文章以增進知識，便於產生力量。尤其，有了好書，更需要身體力行地去認識它、瞭解它、貫通它、融會它，也才能由書中獲益，也才能獲得讀書之樂趣、文飾與能力。

　　本書雖精心編纂，但仍難免有疏漏之處，尚請方家讀者不吝指正。

黃正興　謹誌
2000 年 5 月

Acknowledgement

Talking to People

From *Thinking English* by Michael Thorn, published by Cassell Ltd. in 1982. Reprinted by permission of the publisher.

Thanksgiving Days

From *Autumn Festivals* by Mike Rosen, published by Wayland (Publishers) Limited in 1990. Reprinted by permission of the publisher.

What Happened to the Dinosaurs?

From *Lighthouse English I* published by Kenkyusha Publishing Co., Ltd. Reprinted by permission of the publisher.

The Flower

Written by Pastor John R. Ramsey, published in *A^{2nd} Helping of Chicken Soup for the Soul* by Health Communications, Inc. in 1995. Reprinted by permission of the publisher.

Controlling the Forest

From *A Forest's Life, from Meadow to Mature Woodland* by Cathy Mania and Robert Mania, published by Franklin Watts, a Division of Grolier Publishing in 1997. Reprinted by permission of the publisher.

A Story from Mexico

From *Tales from Many Cultures* by Penny Cameron. Copyright © 1995. Reprinted by permission of Addison Wesley Longman.

Your Personality in the Palm of Your Hand?

From *Scott Foresman English On Target 2* by James E. Purpura & Diane Pinkley. Copyright © 1992. Reprinted by permission of Addison Wesley Longman.

Festivals of New Year

From *Winter Festivals* by Mike Rosen, published by Wayland (Publishers) Limited in 1990. Reprinted by permission of the publisher.

The Day a Mountain Died

From *Composition Practice: Book 4* by Linda Lonon Blanton, published by Heinle & Heinle Publishers in 1993. Reprinted by permission of the publisher.

A Brother Like That

Written by Dan Clark, published in *Chicken Soup for the Soul* by Health Communications, Inc. in 1993. Reprinted by permission of the publisher.

Do-It-Yourself

From *Expressway 4*, 2ⁿᵈ ed. by Steven J. Molinsky and Bill Bliss, © 1997. Reprinted by permission of Prentice-Hall, Inc., Upper Saddle River, NJ.

Chinese New Year Customs

From *Winter Festivals* by Mike Rosen, published by Wayland (Publishers) Limited, 1990. Reprinted by permission of the publisher.

Culture Shock

From *Contact USA*, 3ʳᵈ ed. by Paul Abraham & Daphne Mackey, © 1997. Reprinted by permission of the publisher.

Christmas Traditions

From *Winter Festivals* by Mike Rosen, published by Wayland (Publishers) Limited, 1990. Reprinted by permission of the publisher.

William Shakespeare

Written by Matthew McGinniss.

Helen Keller

Courtesy of the Perkins School for the Blind, Watertown, MA, USA.

新英文選（上）

1 Unit One

Talking to People

1. Is it easy for you to start talking to people?
2. In your country how would you start conversation with a stranger?
3. What are the skills of talking to people?

Johannes had come to England to improve[1] his English. He had studied the language for five years in his own country and he could understand a written[2] text[3] quite well. What he needed *above all* was practice[4] in conversation.

5　　He enrolled[5] at a school for foreign students and the school found him a home with an English family. The family were pleasant and friendly and he was delighted[6] to discover[7] that there was a pretty daughter, only a year *or so* younger than himself. That first night, as he lay in bed, he *was filled with*

10　optimism[8].

　　A few days later, however, when his class teacher, Mr. Price, asked him how he was *getting on*, he had to confess[9] that he felt a little disappointed[10]. 'By Sunday,' said Johannes, 'I'll have been here for two weeks, but I've had very little conversation practice.'

15　　'Aren't you living with an English family?' asked Mr. Price.

　　'Yes, I am,' replied[11] Johannes, 'but they're always busy.'

　　'Aren't there any young people in the family?'

　　'Yes, there's a daughter of 17, but she leaves home at eight o'clock in the morning and she spends every evening with her

20　friends.'

---

1. improve [ɪm'pruv]
2. written ['rɪtn̩]
3. text [tɛkst]
4. practice ['præktɪs]
5. enroll [ɪn'rol]
6. delight [dɪ'laɪt]
7. discover [dɪ'skʌvɚ]
8. optimism ['ɑptə,mɪzəm]
9. confess [kən'fɛs]
10. disappoint [,dɪsə'pɔɪnt]
11. reply [rɪ'plaɪ]

'Well,' said Mr. Price, 'you'll just have to learn to *get into* conversation with strangers.'

'But how?' asked Johannes, 'and where?'

'You travel on buses, don't you?' suggested[12] Mr. Price.

'Yes,' said Johannes doubtfully[13].   25

'Don't sit in an empty[14] seat, sit beside somebody. You can often have marvelous[15] conversations on buses.'

'It's difficult to know what to talk about,' said Johannes. 'That is a problem,' agreed Mr. Price. 'You can always start with the weather, but that won't keep you going for long. You've got to read   30 the papers, watch television, *find out* what English people are talking about. Then after you've talked about the weather, you can ask a question.'

'How do you mean?' Johannes looked puzzled[16].

'Well, let's imagine[17] you read a story in the paper about a   35 murder[18] case or a political[19] election[20]. You could say: "I wonder[21] if they'll find Barrett guilty?" or "Do you think Jordan will win?"—something like that. People like being asked their opinion[22] about things. Or you can try talking about a program you saw on television. "Did you see that play on television last   40

---

12. suggest [səg'dʒɛst]   16. puzzled ['pʌzḷd]   20. election [ɪ'lɛkʃən]
13. doubtfully ['daʊtfəlɪ]   17. imagine [ɪ'mædʒɪn]   21. wonder ['wʌndəˑ]
14. empty ['ɛmptɪ]   18. murder ['mɝˑdəˑ]   22. opinion [ə'pɪnjən]
15. marvelous ['mɑrvḷəs]   19. political [pə'lɪtɪkḷ]

night? Good, wasn't it?" English people won't usually start a conversation, but often they're quite happy to chat[23], provided[24] you start talking to them.'

Johannes nodded[25] 'I see what you mean,' he said thoughtful-
45   ly[26].

'One more thing,' Mr. Price continued, 'older people are nearly always easier to get into conversation with than younger ones. The young *are* terribly[27] wrapped[28] *up in* the their own lives. But the older ones can't resist[29] talking about the good old days. When
50   they were young, the sun was always shining, everybody was always good-humored[30]. There wasn't so much money, but everyone enjoyed themselves. Perhaps it's the same in your country?'

Johannes smiled. 'I think old people are the same all over the
55   world,' he said.

Vocabulary

1. improve [ɪmˈpruv] *vt.* to make something better 改善；提升
   Jim went to America to *improve* his English.

23. chat [tʃæt]
24. provided [prəˈvaɪdɪd]
25. nod [nɑd]
26. thoughtfully [ˈθɔtfəlɪ]

27. terribly [ˈtɛrəblɪ]
28. wrap [ræp]
29. resist [rɪˈzɪst]

30. good-humored
    [ˈɡʊdˈhjumɚd]

2. written ['rɪtn̩] *adj.* 被寫下來的

They put their questions in *written* form.

3. text [tɛkst] *n.* [C][U] the original words and form of a written or printed work 原文

You can find the *text* of "I Have a Dream" through the web easily today.

4. practice ['præktɪs] *n.* [U] repeated and systematic exercise for learning something well 練習

Practice makes perfect.

5. enroll [ɪn'rol] *vi., vt.* to insert, register, or enter in a list, catalog, or roll 登記；註冊

Jane *enrolled* at an American school last week.

6. delight [dɪ'laɪt] *vi., vt.* to give joy or satisfaction to 使高興，使快樂

We were *delighted* to meet them at the airport.

7. discover [dɪ'skʌvɚ] *vt.* to find out 發現

I was happy to *discover* that they had a little dog.

8. optimism ['ɑptə,mɪzəm] *n.* [U] a tendency to expect the best possible outcome on the most hopeful aspects of a situation 樂觀；樂觀主義 (↔ pessimism)

Alice's heart is full of *optimism* and she always looks on the bright side of things.

9. confess [kən'fɛs] *vi., vt.* to admit 坦承，承認

He *confessed* that he made many mistakes.

10. disappoint [,dɪsə'pɔɪnt] *vt.* to frustrate 使失望；使沮喪

The players felt a little *disappointed* at the game.

11. reply [rɪ'plaɪ] *vi., vt.* to respond in words or writing 答覆

He *replied* to me in a loud voice.

12. suggest [səg'dʒɛst] *vt.* to propose 建議

I *suggest* he travel on buses.

13. doubtfully ['dautfəlɪ] *adv.* uncertainly 懷疑地；缺乏自信地

The student answered his teacher's question *doubtfully*.

14. empty ['ɛmptɪ] *adj.* not occupied 空的

There are many *empty* houses on this island.

15. marvelous ['mɑrvḷəs] *adj.* astonishing 令人驚奇的

It's *marvelous* that the bird should disappear in the magician's hat.

16. puzzled ['pʌzḷd] *adj.* confused 困惑的

Jim looked *puzzled* at this question.

17. imagine [ɪ'mædʒɪn] *vt.* to suppose 想像

The child *imagined* that he could fly.

18. murder ['mɝdɚ] *n.* C U the unlawful killing of a person 謀殺

A *murder* case happened last night.

19. political [pə'lɪtɪkḷ] *adj.* of politics 政治的

KMT and DPP are *political* parties.

20. election [ɪ'lɛkʃən] *n.* C U an act or process of electing 選舉

A presidential *election* was held in Taiwan on the 18th of March, 2000.

21. wonder ['wʌndɚ] *vi., vt.* to be curious about 想知道；對…感到好奇

I *wonder* if it will be fine tomorrow.

22. opinion [ə'pɪnjən] *n.* C U a view, judgment, or belief 意見

In my *opinion*, you are right.

23. chat [tʃæt] *vi.* to talk in an informal or familiar manner 閒聊

They are happy to *chat* with you.

24. provided [prə'vaɪdɪd] *conj.* if 假如

We will travel *provided* it is fine tomorrow.

25. nod [nɑd] *vi., vt.* 點頭

The girl *nodded* her head.

26. thoughtfully [ˈθɔtfəlɪ] *adv.* deeply absorbed in thought 沈思地

    He looked at the painting *thoughtfully*.

27. terribly [ˈtɛrəblɪ] *adv.* very, extremely 非常

    That mother is *terribly* worried about her children's health.

28. wrap [ræp] *vt.* to cover something in a material folded around 包；裹

    Sara is *wrapped* up in listening to the radio.

29. resist [rɪˈzɪst] *vi., vt.* to stand 忍受；抵抗

    The dog *resisted* going with the boy.

30. good-humored [ˈgʊdˈhjuməd] *adj.* cheerful 心情愉快的

    You are *good-humored* today.

Idioms and Phrases

1. above all 尤其

   What we need *above all* is clean air.

2. or so 大約

   The girl is two years *or so* younger than I.

3. be filled with... 充滿…

   His eyes *are filled with* hope.

4. get on 進展，進步

   He is *getting on* well in America.

5. get into... 開始…

   Lisa finds it easy to *get into* conversation with others.

6. find out 發現

   She tried to *find out* what the sign meant.

7. be wrapped up in... 埋首於…，熱中於…

   Helen *is wrapped up in* music.

Exercise

I True or False

( ) 1. Johannes had come to America to improve his English.

( ) 2. What Johannes needed above all was practice in writing.

( ) 3. Johannes enrolled in a school for local students.

( ) 4. The school found him a home with an English family.

( ) 5. The family were pleasant and friendly.

( ) 6. The first night when he was in that new family he was filled with fear.

( ) 7. At first, Johannes had much conversation practice.

( ) 8. In the family there was a daughter of 19.

( ) 9. People can always start conversation with the weather.

( ) 10. Old people are happy to chat all over the world.

II Reading Comprehension

1. Why did Johannes come to England?

2. How long had Johannes studied English in his own country?

3. Why did Johannes feel a little disappointed when Mr. Price asked him how he was going on? So what did Mr. Price suggest?

4. What steps does Mr. Price advise Johannes to take for finding suitable topics of conversation?

5. What method does Mr. Price suggest for actually starting the conversation?

III Discussion

1. Do you think Mr. Price is correct in his suggestions?

2. Do you think the advice Mr. Price gives Johannes would be suitable for a girl? Give your reasons.

3. If you were Johannes, how would you start a nice conversation with the "pretty daughter"? (Try to be specific and arrange a step-by-step procedure.)

4. Do you think that old people are the same all over the world? Why or why not?

IV Vocabulary Selection

(　　) 1. Johannes had come to England to _____ his English.

    (A) improve　(B) suggest　(C) confess

(　　) 2. Columbus _____ America in 1492.

    (A) agreed　(B) discovered　(C) traveled

(　　) 3. Father looked _____ at his son's strange question.

    (A) started　(B) puzzled　(C) nodded

(　　) 4. They will be happy to chat _____ you start first.

    (A) confessed　(B) wrapped　(C) provided

(　　) 5. He was unable to _____ laughing at the show.

    (A) resist　(B) reply　(C) shine

(　　) 6. Long time ago people _____ that they could fly.

    (A) delighted　(B) wondered　(C) imagined

(　　) 7. _____ makes perfect.

    (A) Improvement　(B) Practice　(C) Election

(　　) 8. All the audience left, but he still _____ talking.

(A) continued　(B) disappointed　(C) chatted

(　) 9. Linda _____ at a famous university in the U.S.

(A) enrolled　(B) seated　(C) murdered

(　) 10. When the man was found _____, he cried.

(A) thoughtful　(B) empty　(C) guilty

Ⅴ Word Forms

Verb	Noun	Adjective
practice	practice	practical
please	pleasure	pleasant
–	friend	friendly
delight	delight	delightful
discover	discovery	–
confess	confess	confessed
disappoint	disappointment	disappointed
suggest	suggestion	suggestive
terrify	terror	terrible
continue	continuation	continuous

1. Nowadays people like to learn _____ (practice) knowledge.

2. It was a _____ (pleasure) trip to go to Macao.

3. The ship is going to make a _____ (friend) tour.

4. To enjoy fresh fruit is very _____ (delight).

5. His _____ (discover) of new methods is marvelous.

6. He stood _____ (confess) for what he had done.

7. The coach was much _____ (disappoint) at the players.

8. We took his _____ (suggest) and stayed there.

9. A _____ (terror) typhoon attacked the city.

10. Despite the noise, the speaker _____ (continue) talking.

VI Idioms and Phrases

(*Make any change in verb forms, if necessary.*)

above all	lie in bed	on buses	talk about
start with	for long	find out	provided
be wrapped up in	be filled with		

1. The jazz singers will come _____ it is fine here.

2. Lisa has _____ arts since childhood.

3. During earthquakes, people _____ fear.

4. Dan likes to start conversation _____.

5. Bill sat up late and is now _____.

6. They are movie fans. They like to _____ movie stars.

7. _____, I like to eat Italian food.

8. For need of money, the business won't go on _____.

9. In conversation, people usually _____ the weather.

10. The scientists will _____ the truth about nature.

VII Matching

_____ 1. You can try talking about   a. but everybody enjoyed themselves.

_____ 2. Johannes had to confess   b. a program you saw on TV.

_____ 3. The young are terribly   c. if they'll find Barrett guilty.

_____ 4. I wonder

d. he was filled with optimism.

_____ 5. There wasn't much money,

e. that he felt disappointed.

_____ 6. As he lay in bed,

f. wrapped up in their own lives.

VIII Cloze Test

The young _____1_____ terribly wrapped _____2_____ in _____3_____ own lives. But the older _____4_____ can't resist _____5_____ about the good old _____6_____. When they _____7_____ young, the sun _____8_____ always shining, everybody _____9_____ always good-humored.

( ) 1. (A) can (B) are (C) is (D) be

( ) 2. (A) to (B) up (C) on (D) down

( ) 3. (A) their (B) his (C) its (D) one's

( ) 4. (A) one (B) ones (C) one's (D) once

( ) 5. (A) talk (B) to talk (C) talking (D) talked

( ) 6. (A) sky (B) smiles (C) men (D) days

( ) 7. (A) were (B) was (C) are (D) is

( ) 8. (A) is (B) are (C) was (D) were

( ) 9. (A) is (B) are (C) were (D) was

IX Translation

1. 年紀大的人幾乎總比年紀輕的人容易打開話匣子。年輕人是非常專注於他們自己的生活。

   Older people _____ nearly always easier to _____ into _____ with than _____ ones. The young _____ terribly _____ up in their own _____.

2. 那兒沒有很多錢，但每個人都很自得其樂。或許在你們國家亦然？我想世界
   各地老人都是一樣的。

   There _____ so much money, but everyone _____ themselves.
   _____ it's the _____ in your _____? I think old _____
   are the same all _____ the _____.

X Grammar

Pronoun 代名詞 (Pron.)

*定義：代名詞是用以代替名詞的字。

*種類：通常分為下列五種：

人稱代名詞	I, you, he, she, etc.
指示代名詞	this, that, those, etc.
不定代名詞	one, some, all, etc.
疑問代名詞	who, what, which, etc.
關係代名詞	who, which, what, etc.

*主要的人稱代名詞如下：

		主格	所有格	受格	所有格代名詞
第一人稱	單數	I	my	me	mine
	複數	we	our	us	ours
第二人稱	單數	you	your	you	yours
	複數	you	your	you	yours
第三人稱	單數	he she it	his her its	him her it	his hers its
	複數	they	their	them	theirs

Focus 1.1.1

請在 A, B, C, D 中選出一個最符合題句的正確答案。

(　) "Do you see all your friends here?" "Everyone except _____."

(A) he　(B) it　(C) his　(D) him

〈解析〉1. 介系詞後接名詞或代名詞之受格。

　　　　e.g. He is looking at me.

　　　2. "except" 為介系詞。

〈Ans〉D

Focus 1.1.2

請在 A, B, C, D 中選出一個最符合題句的正確答案。

(　) The school found _____ a home with an English family.

(A) he　(B) him　(C) his　(D) she

〈解析〉1. 動詞的受詞用受格。

　　　　e.g. He saw me.

　　　2. "him" 為動詞 "found" 之受詞。

〈Ans〉B

Focus 1.1.3

請在 A, B, C, D 中選出一個最符合題句的正確答案。

(　) She spends every evening with _____ friends.

(A) she　(B) he　(C) her　(D) him

〈解析〉1. 所有格後接名詞。

　　　　e.g. my friend, his dog, our school

　　　2. 只有 "her" 為所有格。

〈Ans〉C

Focus 1.1.4

請在 A, B, C, D 中選出一個最符合題句的正確答案。

(　) People like being asked _____ opinion about things.

(A) his　(B) their　(C) one's　(D) him

〈解析〉1. 所有格必須與其先行之主詞一致。

e.g. I love my family.

He has his bicycle.

2. 主詞為 "people" 所以其所有格為 "their"。

〈Ans〉B

Focus 1.2.1

請在 A, B, C, D 中找出一個不符合正確語法的錯誤之處。

(　) In the early morning the first thing that both my brother and me
　　　　　(A)　　　　　　　　　　　　　(B)　　　　　　　(C)

did was to go out to see the pony.
(D)

〈解析〉子句的主詞為主格："my brother and I" 為 "that" 子句裏的主詞，所

以要用主格 "I"。

〈Ans〉C, me → I

Focus 1.2.2

請在 A, B, C, D 中找出一個不符合正確語法的錯誤之處。

(　) He was delighted to discover that there was a pretty daughter, only
　　　　　　(A)　　　　　　　　　　　　　　　　　　(B)

a year or so younger than herself.
(C)　　　　　　　　(D)

〈解析〉反身受詞必須與先行之主詞一致。

e.g. He said to himself.

She expressed herself.

〈Ans〉D, herself → himself

Focus 1.2.3

請在 A, B, C, D 中找出一個不符合正確語法的錯誤之處。

(　) Often they're quite happy to chat, provided you start talking to
　　　　　　　　　 (A)　　　　　　 (B)　　　　　　　　 (C)

him.
(D)

〈解析〉受格必須與先行之主詞一致。

e.g. They wanted us to respect them.

He asked me to write him a letter.

〈Ans〉D, him → them

XI Short Story

Thanksgiving Days

When the first Europeans settled in America they arrived too late to sow crops for the following year's harvest. Nearly half the settlers died of starvation during that first winter. The next spring, those who had survived were able to plant their seeds and, after an excellent summer harvest, they celebrated with a festival. The festival became known as Thanksgiving Day, and in 1941 it was given the fixed date each year of the fourth Thursday in November.

Food is an important part of Thanksgiving celebrations. Traditional thanksgiving foods include turkey, which is eaten with cranberry sauce, and pumpkin pie. At Thanksgiving, as many of the family as possible will gather together. Like many other public holidays, Thanksgiving is often celebrated with street parties and sporting events.

Thanksgiving is also celebrated in Canada, where it is held on the second Monday in October. Canadians hold Thanksgiving before the Americans because winter begins earlier in Canada than the USA.

In Japan, one of the most important harvests is that of the autumn rice crop. Traditionally, none of the newly-grown rice could be eaten until a ceremony had been held to honor the spirits which were thought to protect the rice while it grew. There was a procession and a great banquet, at which ceremonial dances were performed. At midnight, the Emperor of Japan took part in a ritual, presenting a portion of the harvest at a sacred altar. Today the festival is a public holiday, when people celebrate the success of Japanese industry and farming. It is called Labor Thanksgiving Day.

XII Poem

Second Farewell to Cambridge
−Hsu Chih-Mo
Gently I left,
As gently I came;
Slowly I waved my hand,
Saying farewell to cloud in western sky.
Quietly I left,
As quietly I came;

再別康橋
——徐志摩
輕輕的我走了，
正如我輕輕的來；
我輕輕的招手，
作別西天的雲彩。
悄悄的我走了，
正如我悄悄的來；

Unit 1 Exercise

Smartly I fluttered my sleeves,
Taking away nothing even a rosy cloud.

我揮一揮衣袖，
不帶走一片雲彩。

作者簡介：

徐志摩 (Hsu Chih-Mo) (1896–1931)

浙江硤石鎮人，家境富裕，才氣橫溢，惜英年遽逝，壯志未酬，享齡三十五歲。
一九二〇年畢業於美國紐約哥倫比亞大學獲碩士學位。其作品風格有時豪放不
羈，熱情奔放；有時愁雲密佈，悱惻動人；有時慷慨陳辭，意境高深。

XIII Words Review

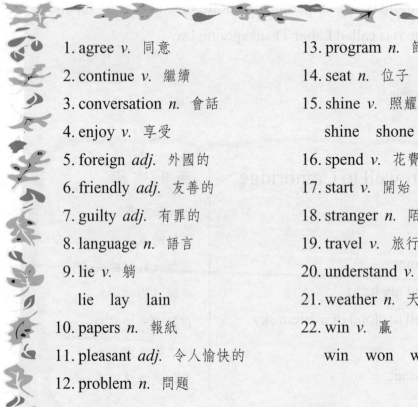

1. agree v. 同意
2. continue v. 繼續
3. conversation n. 會話
4. enjoy v. 享受
5. foreign adj. 外國的
6. friendly adj. 友善的
7. guilty adj. 有罪的
8. language n. 語言
9. lie v. 躺
   lie   lay   lain
10. papers n. 報紙
11. pleasant adj. 令人愉快的
12. problem n. 問題

13. program n. 節目
14. seat n. 位子
15. shine v. 照耀
    shine   shone   shone
16. spend v. 花費
17. start v. 開始
18. stranger n. 陌生人
19. travel v. 旅行
20. understand v. 了解
21. weather n. 天氣
22. win v. 贏
    win   won   won

2 Unit Two

What Happened to the Dinosaurs?

1. What are dinosaurs? Are they all very big?
2. Have you ever seen dinosaurs? If so, where?
3. Are there still many dinosaurs alive?

A hundred million years ago, in the age when there were no human[1] beings, many kinds of dinosaurs[2] ruled[3] the earth. Some were very large and were 30 meters long. *Of course*, there are no dinosaurs on the earth now. They suddenly *died out* about 65 million years ago. But why did they all die? Although no one knows the answer to this question, various[4] opinions have been offered[5].

Scientists *in the past* said that dinosaurs grew *too* large *to* live on the earth, or that they were beaten[6] and killed by higher and stronger animals, *that is*, mammals[7]. Many scientists say today, however[8], that they died because the climate and their environment[9] greatly changed, and therefore it became impossible for them to live on the earth. But, what caused this change?

Some scientists believe[10] that they became extinct[11] when a giant meteorite[12] hit[13] the earth. This meteorite was perhaps[14] 10 kilometers wide and weighed[15] more than a hundred billion tons. This is much larger and heavier than Mt. Everest. When the meteorite hit the earth, it caused an explosion[16] a million times

1. human [ˈhjumən]
2. dinosaur [ˈdaɪnəˌsɔr]
3. rule [rul]
4. various [ˈvɛrɪəs]
5. offer [ˈɔfɚ]
6. beat [bit]
7. mammal [ˈmæml̩]
8. however [haʊˈɛvɚ]
9. environment [ɪnˈvaɪrənmənt]
10. believe [bəˈliv]
11. extinct [ɪkˈstɪŋkt]
12. meteorite [ˈmitɪɚˌaɪt]
13. hit [hɪt]
14. perhaps [pɚˈhæps]
15. weigh [we]
16. explosion [ɪkˈsploʒən]

greater than that of the largest man-made[17] bomb[18]. A huge cloud of dust[19] *was thrown*[20] *up into* the air by this explosion and covered the earth for several years. The rays[21] of the sun were blocked[22] by this cloud, and no sunshine could reach the surface of the earth. First the plants died, and then the dinosaurs and other animals that ate the plants also died. Finally, the meat-eating[23] dinosaurs that ate the weaker animals died.

　　Dinosaurs were the kings of the animals *at that time*, but they were not able to live after this great change in their environment. Such an environmental change can be caused by nuclear[24] explosions, too. *In fact*, the theory that a meteorite explosion *killed off* the dinosaurs helped to shape[25] the concept[26] of "*nuclear winter*."

20

25

30

Vocabulary

1. human [ˈhjumən] *n.* C human being 人類
   Human beings should love each other.
2. dinosaur [ˈdaɪnəˌsɔr] *n.* C an extremely large reptile that lived in very ancient times and disappeared suddenly 恐龍
   Dinosaurs disappeared from the earth.

17. man-made [ˈmænˈmed]	20. throw [θro]	[ˈmitˌɪtɪŋ]
18. bomb [bɑm]	21. ray [re]	24. nuclear [ˈnjuklɪ♂]
19. dust [dʌst]	22. block [blɑk]	25. shape [ʃep]
	23. meat-eating	26. concept [ˈkɑnsɛpt]

3. rule [rul] *vi., vt.* to control   統治；管理

The king used to *rule* the kingdom.

4. various [ˈvɛrɪəs] *adj.* several   各種的

There are *various* answers to a question.

5. offer [ˈɔfɚ] *vt.* to provide, give   提供

They *offer* good services for people.

6. beat [bit] *vi., vt.* to defeat   打敗

The boxer was *beaten* at once.

7. mammal [ˈmæml] *n.* C an animal which is fed on milk from the mother's body when young   哺乳動物

Men are a kind of *mammal*.

Most *mammals* are four-footed.

8. however [haʊˈɛvɚ] *conj.* but   然而，可是

9. environment [ɪnˈvaɪrənmənt] *n.* C U the natural conditions, such as air, water, and land, in which people, animals, and plants live   環境

The school offers very good learning *environments*.

10. believe [bəˈliv] *vi., vt.* to consider to be true, honest or real   相信

It is not good to *believe* everything you hear.

11. extinct [ɪkˈstɪŋkt] *adj.* no longer existing   絕種的，滅絕的

Many animals have become *extinct*.

12. meteorite [ˈmitɪəˌaɪt] *n.* C a meteor that has landed on the Earth, without being totally burnt up   隕石

The *meteorite* hit the earth.

13. hit [hɪt] *vt.* to come against with force   撞上；打中

Our car was *hit* by a motorcycle.

14. perhaps [pɚˈhæps] *adv.* maybe   大概，可能

I found *perhaps* ten students in the classroom.

15. weigh [we] *vi., vt.* to have a certain weight 重

    The dinosaur *weighed* about 1,000 pounds.

16. explosion [ɪkˈsploʒən] *n.* C an act of exploding 爆炸

    The *explosion* has caused much damage.

17. man-made [ˈmænˈmed] *adj.* produced by people 人造的

    This is a kind of *man-made* fibre.

    There are many *man-made* satellites in the space.

18. bomb [bɑm] *n.* C an explosive device 炸彈

    The fire caused the explosion of the *bombs*.

19. dust [dʌst] *n.* U finely powdered earth 灰塵

20. throw [θro] *vt.* to send with force 丟，擲

    A ball was *thrown* up into the air by the boy.

21. ray [re] *n.* C a narrow beam of light 光線

22. block [blɑk] *vt.* to prevent movement through 阻礙；阻塞

    The traffic was *blocked* by the parade.

    The streets were *blocked* by the accident.

23. meat-eating [ˈmitˌɪtɪŋ] *adj.* 肉食的

    Some dinosaurs are *meat-eating* animals.

24. nuclear [ˈnjuklɪɚ] *adj.* of, concerning or using nuclear energy 核子的

    Nuclear wars should be prevented.

25. shape [ʃep] *vi., vt.* to make or form 形成

    Education will help students *shape* good concepts.

    The ladies are in good *shape*.

26. concept [ˈkɑnsɛpt] *n.* C a thought, idea, or principle 觀念；概念

    Good *concepts* will lead to good actions.

Idioms and Phrases

1. of course　當然

   Of course, I believe what you say.

2. die out　滅亡；滅絕

   Many animals *died out* long time ago.

3. in the past　在過去

   Scientists *in the past* made many important discoveries.

4. too...to...　太…而不能…

   Dinosaurs grew *too* large *to* live on the earth.

   He was *too* busy *to* come to see us.

5. that is　也就是說

   The dog is very obedient, *that is*, doing everything as I say.

6. be thrown up into...　被拋到…

   The roof *was thrown up into* the sky by the explosion.

7. at that time　那時

   I was very nervous *at that time*.

   They were frightened *at that time*.

8. in fact　事實上

   In fact, the judge tells the truth.

9. kill off　滅絕；殺光

   The insecticide *kills off* all the insects.

   The farmer *killed off* all the flies.

10. nuclear winter　核子冬天（核戰之後所引起的地球寒冷化現象）

Exercise

I True or False

(   ) 1. A hundred million years ago, many kinds of dinosaurs ruled the earth.

(   ) 2. Some dinosaurs were very large and were 300 meters long.

(   ) 3. There are some dinosaurs on the earth now.

(   ) 4. Dinosaurs grew too small to live on the earth.

(   ) 5. Maybe dinosaurs died because the climate changed.

(   ) 6. Some believe they became extinct when a giant meteorite hit the earth.

(   ) 7. When the meteorite hit the earth, it caused a great explosion.

(   ) 8. After the explosion, a huge cloud of dust covered the earth for few minutes.

(   ) 9. After the explosion, the sun still shone and there was sunshine on the earth.

(   ) 10. Dinosaurs were the kings of the animals at that time.

II Reading Comprehension

1. Who ruled the earth a hundred million years ago?

2. Are there still any dinosaurs now?

3. When did the dinosaurs suddenly die out?

4. What did scientists in the past say about dinosaurs?

5. What do many scientists today say about dinosaurs?

6. What do some scientists believe?

7. Who were the kings of the animals at that time?

8. What helped to shape the concept of "nuclear winter"?

III Discussion

1. From the food they eat, what are the two kinds of dinosaurs?

2. What do dinosaurs look like? Discuss and draw a picture, if possible.

3. Why do you think dinosaurs died out?

4. Why are dinosaurs still very popular now? Discuss and write down the reasons.

IV Vocabulary Selection

(　　) 1. In my _____, I don't agree with him on this point.
   (A) climate　(B) opinion　(C) environment

(　　) 2. Environmental _____ is an important topic now.
   (A) nuclear　(B) surface　(C) protection

(　　) 3. The _____ of the bombs caused many broken houses.
   (A) concept　(B) explosion　(C) shape

(　　) 4. The parade was _____ by the traffic accident.
   (A) blocked　(B) weighed　(C) covered

(　　) 5. The _____ of her skin is very smooth.
   (A) surface　(B) color　(C) ray

(　　) 6. Good education has _____ his correct concepts.
   (A) man-made　(B) thrown　(C) shaped

(　　) 7. Many rare animals have become _____ now.

(A) human   (B) extinct   (C) heavy

( ) 8. She has no _____ to complain about living.

(A) cause   (B) cloud   (C) theory

( ) 9. Out of joy the winner _____ up his hat into the sky.

(A) offered   (B) reached   (C) threw

( ) 10. The boxer was _____ in the third round.

(A) ruled   (B) beaten   (C) weighed

Ⅴ Word Forms

Verb	Noun	Adjective
explode	explosion	explosive
rule	rule	–
weigh	weight	weighing
theorize	theory	theoretical
–	concept	conceptual
–	extinction	extinct
–	various	variety
–	dust	dusty
–	cloud	cloudy
finalize	final	final

1. The bombs _____ (explode) and destroyed the house.

2. The king _____ (rule) the country for twenty years.

3. The _____ (weigh) of the lady is known to everyone.

4. The teacher's lecture is too much _____ (theory).

5. He tried to answer a _____ (concept) question.

6. The _____ (extinct) of the lights left the room in darkness.

7. The vender sells _____ (variety) kinds of toys.

8. The streets sometimes were very _____ (dust).

9. A _____ (cloud) day is good for picnicking.

10. This is our _____ (final) day at school.

VI Idioms and Phrases

(*Make any change in verb forms, if necessary.*)

on the earth	on earth	in the past	that is
able to	be thrown up into	in fact	kill off
although	die out		

1. Many old customs will gradually _____.

2. What _____ are you talking about?

3. _____, I don't believe what he said.

4. The country produces black gold, _____, oil.

5. _____ the desert was a beautiful meadow.

6. The clerk said that he was not _____ come.

7. The buffalo _____ the sky by a tornado.

8. _____ he set out late, he arrived early.

9. Whales are the largest animals _____.

10. The medicine will _____ all the germs.

VII Matching

_____ 1. A hundred million years ago,   a. helped to shape the concept of

_____ 2. The rays of the sun were   "nuclear winter."

_____ 3. Although no one knows the   b. about 65 million years ago.

answer,   c. it caused a very great explosion.

_____ 4. The theory that a meteorite d. there were no human beings.

explosion killed off the   e. various opinions have been

dinosaurs   offered.

_____ 5. They suddenly died out   f. blocked by this cloud.

_____ 6. When the meteorite hit the

earth,

VIII Cloze Test

Many scientists ____1____ today, however, that they ____2____ because the

____3____ and their ____4____ greatly ____5____ , and ____6____ it

became ____7____ for ____8____ to live ____9____ the earth.

( ) 1. (A) say   (B) beat   (C) offer   (D) rule

( ) 2. (A) died   (B) killed   (C) grew   (D) ate

( ) 3. (A) plant   (B) cause   (C) meteorite   (D) climate

( ) 4. (A) sunshine   (B) environment   (C) mammal   (D) concept

( ) 5. (A) weighed   (B) beaten   (C) changed   (D) reached

( ) 6. (A) but   (B) therefore   (C) never   (D) ever

( ) 7. (A) natural   (B) possible   (C) impossible   (D) heavy

( ) 8. (A) it   (B) they   (C) them   (D) him

( ) 9. (A) in   (B) on   (C) to   (D) for

IX Translation

1. 太陽光被塵雲所阻擋，沒有陽光可以到達地球表面。一開始植物死了，然後吃植物的恐龍及其他動物也死了。

The rays of the _____ were _____ by this _____, and no _____ could reach the _____ of the _____. First the _____ died, and then the _____ and other _____ that _____ the plants also died.

2. 那時候，恐龍是動物的國王，但在牠們的環境經歷此一巨大的改變後，牠們已無法生存。

Dinosaurs were the _____ of the _____ at _____ time, but they were not _____ to _____ after this great _____ in their _____.

X Grammar

Conjunction 連接詞 (Conj.)

*定義：連接詞連接兩個相對稱的字、詞、子句或句子。

*常用的連接詞有：

按功用分	對等連接詞	and, but, or , for, nor, etc.
	從屬連接詞	because, until, that, when, where, why, who, whom, how, what, etc.
按形式分	單一連接詞	and, but, or, after, if, etc.
	片語連接詞	as well as, as if, etc.
	相關連接詞	both...and, either...or, etc.

Focus 2.1.1

請在 A, B, C, D 中選出一個最符合題句的正確答案。

(　) A knot is joining two pieces of rope _____ of cord.

　　(A) with　(B) or　(C) because　(D) where

〈解析〉連接詞連接兩個相對稱的字、詞、子句或句子。

　　　　e.g. I like dancing and swimming.

　　　　　　 I think that he is right and that he will come.

　　　　　　 I met them and they smiled at me.

　　　　　　 I will use a pen or a pencil.

　　　　＊因 "of rope" 與 "of cord" 對稱，所以選連接詞 "or"。

〈Ans〉B

Focus 2.1.2

請在 A, B, C, D 中選出一個最符合題句的正確答案。

(　) Some dinosaurs were very large _____ were 30 meters long.

　　(A) but　(B) and　(C) or　(D) if

〈解析〉如果選項皆為對等連接詞，就要看文章之上下意思來決定。

　　　　e.g. "and" 前後意思「一致」

　　　　　　 "but" 前後意思「相反」

　　　　　　 "or" 前後意思「可替用」

　　　　＊因屬一致性的：前為 "large"，後為 "long"，故選 "and"。

〈Ans〉B

Focus 2.1.3

請在 A, B, C, D 中選出一個最符合題句的正確答案。

(　) Scientists in the past said _____ dinosaurs grew too large to live on the earth.

(A) that　(B) what　(C) where　(D) who

〈解析〉"that" 的功用為將主要子句與陳述一件事情的附屬子句連接起來。

e.g. He said that I was right.

We hope that we will win the race.

〈Ans〉A

Focus 2.2.1

請在 A, B, C, D 中找出一個不符合正確語法的錯誤之處。

(　) Professor Duncan teaches both anthropology as well as sociology
　　　　　　　　　(A)　(B)　　(C)

each fall.
(D)

〈解析〉連接詞不能重複使用。

e.g. I like both apples and lemons.

I like apples as well as lemons.

但不能一起用成 "both...as well as"。

〈Ans〉B, both 去掉

Focus 2.2.2

請在 A, B, C, D 中找出一個不符合正確語法的錯誤之處。

(　) Many scientists say that dinosaurs died because of the climate and
　　　　　　　　　(A)　　　(B)　　　　　(C)

their environment greatly changed.
(D)

〈解析〉"because of" 與 "because" 的用法：

"because of" 後要接「名詞」或「名詞片語」。

"because" 後要接「子句」。

〈Ans〉C, because of → because

Focus 2.2.3

請在 A, B, C, D 中找出一個不符合正確語法的錯誤之處。

(　) A huge <u>cloud of dust</u> <u>was thrown up</u> into the air <u>by this explosion</u>
　　　　　　(A)　　　　　　(B)　　　　　　　　　(C)
and <u>covering</u> the earth for several years.
　　　(D)

〈解析〉連接詞所連接的字、詞、子句、句子，要有「一致性」與「對稱性」。

e.g. He came here and picked us up.

不能用 He came here and picking us up.

〈Ans〉D, covering → covered

XI Short Story

The Flower

For some time I have had a person provide me with a rose boutonniere to pin on the lapel of my suit every Sunday. Because I always got a flower on Sunday morning, I really did not think much of it. It was a nice gesture that I appreciated, but it became routine. One Sunday, however, what I considered ordinary became very special.

As I was leaving the Sunday service a young man approached me. He walked right up to me and said, "Sir, what are you going to do with your flower?" At first I did not know what he was talking about, but then I understood.

I said, "Do you mean this?" as I pointed to the rose pinned to my coat.

He said, "Yes sir. I would like it if you are just going to throw it away." At this point I smiled and gladly told him that he could have my flower, casually asking him what he was going to do with it. The little boy, who was probably less than 10 years old, looked up at me and said, "Sir, I'm going to give it to my granny. My mother and father got divorced last year. I was living with my mother, but when she married again, she wanted me to live with my father. I lived with him for a while, but he said I could not stay, so he sent me to live with my grandmother. She is so good to me. She cooks for me and takes care of me. She has been so good to me that I want to give that pretty flower to her for loving me."

When the little boy finished I could hardly speak. My eyes filled with tears and I knew I had been touched in the depths of my soul. I reached up and unpinned my flower. With the flower in my hand, I looked at the boy and said, "Son, that is the nicest thing I have ever heard, but you can't have this flower because it's not enough. If you'll look in front of the pulpit, you'll see a big bouquet of flowers. Different families buy them for the church each week. Please take those flowers to your granny because she deserves the very best."

If I hadn't been touched enough already, he made one last statement and I will always cherish it. He said, "What a wonderful day! I asked for one flower but got a beautiful bouquet."

XII Poem

When We Two Parted

–George Gordon Byron

When we two parted

In silence and tears,

Half broken-hearted,

To sever for years,

Pale grew thy cheek and cold,

Colder thy kiss;

Truly that hour foretold

Sorrow to this!

猶憶訣別時

——拜倫

猶憶訣別時

無言共涕泣,

幾已達心碎,

分別要多年,

蒼涼紅顏白,

吻別猶悽切;

往日言成真

今朝愁別離!

Rhyme-scheme: a b a b c d c d

作者簡介:

George Gordon Byron (拜倫) (1788–1824)

為英國浪漫時期文學史上,享有國際盛名的一位詩人。

拜倫英俊瀟灑,多情善感,抱負不凡。慷慨激昂,熱愛自由,痛恨暴政。甚至不惜冒著生命危險,為被壓迫者挺身奮鬥。他幫助希臘脫離土耳其的專制統治而獨立,成為希臘人民景仰的革命英雄。

拜倫注重內容及情感的表露。其作品自創一格,蒼勁生動,充滿情感。因他較能選擇適當的題材,並運用豐富的想像力,其作品產生的強大吸引力,使他在國際上立下不可動搖的地位。

Unit 2 Exercise

XIII Words Review

1. although *conj.* 雖然
2. billion *n.* 十億
3. cause *v.* 引起
4. change *n.* 變化
5. climate *n.* 氣候
6. cover *v.* 覆蓋
7. earth *n.* 地球
8. giant *adj.* 巨大的
9. grow *v.* 成長
10. heavy *adj.* 重的
11. impossible *adj.* 不可能的
12. kilometer *n.* 公里
13. meter *n.* 公尺
14. million *n.* 百萬
15. reach *v.* 到達
16. suddenly *adv.* 突然
17. surface *n.* 表面
18. theory *n.* 理論
19. time *n.* 倍
20. ton *n.* 噸
21. weak *adj.* 虛弱的

3

Controlling the Forest

1. What is a forest? Are there many trees in it?
2. Are there many forests in your country?
3. Is your country controlling the forest? If so, why?

A forest's natural[1] cycle[2] of growth and development[3] will continue uninterrupted[4] — unless[5] people do something to stop it. Have you ever mowed[6] a lawn or pulled "weeds" out of a garden? By cutting the grass or removing certain plants from a

5　plot[7] of land, you were stopping the forest at a very early stage[8] in its development.

Besides[9] preventing[10] a forest *from* growing, people can also choose the type of forest that grows in a particular[11] area. *For example*, in the southeastern[12] part of the United States, people

10　prevent intermediate[13] pine forests from developing into mature[14] broadleaf[15] forests by occasionally[16] setting small fires that kill the young broadleaf trees. The people who own the land prefer[17] pine forests because pines grow faster and can be used to make paper, furniture, and other products.

15　These forests must be closely managed[18] to successfully disrupt[19] the forest's natural recovery[20] cycle. Despite[21] human

....

1. natural ['næt ʃərəl]
2. cycle ['saɪkl]
3. development
　[dɪ'vɛləpmənt]
4. uninterrupted
　[ˌʌnɪntə'rʌptɪd]
5. unless [ən'lɛs]
6. mow [mo]
7. plot [plɑt]

8. stage [stedʒ]
9. besides [bɪ'saɪdz]
10. prevent [prɪ'vɛnt]
11. particular [pə'tɪkjələ]
12. southeastern
　[ˌsauθ'istən]
13. intermediate
　[ˌɪntə'midɪɪt]
14. mature [mə'tjʊr]

15. broadleaf ['brɔd,lif]
16. occasionally
　[ə'keʒənlɪ]
17. prefer [prɪ'fɝ]
18. manage ['mænɪdʒ]
19. disrupt [dɪs'rʌpt]
20. recovery [rɪ'kʌvərɪ]
21. despite [dɪ'spaɪt]

attempts[22] to prevent broadleaf trees from growing, oaks, hickories, and other broadleaf trees often manage to grow fairly large. Trying to *keep* broadleaf trees *from* growing in these forests is as much trouble as *keeping* weeds[23] *out of* a flower garden.   20

In recent years, many forest scientists have begun to understand that *putting out* natural wildfires[24] in national parks and national forests also affects[25] what type of forest grows in an area. Many now feel that natural fires—like the fires that destroyed[26] much of Yellowstone National Park in 1988—should   25 be allowed to burn.

The lodgepole pine, which is common in Yellowstone National Park, is an example of a tree that needs fire to reproduce[27]. Its cones do not *open up* until they are heated. Also, fire clears the undergrowth[28], *making room for* the seedlings[29] to grow. Without   30 fire, the lodgepole pines in this forest would be replaced[30] by spruce, fir, or other trees.

Whether a forest is burned or cut down, it will come back. It's hard to *stop* a forest *from* developing. *As long as* the soil remains[31] and there is enough rainfall[32], the process[33] of recovery begins   35

22. attempt [ə'tɛmpt]
23. weed [wid]
24. wildfire ['waɪld‚faɪr]
25. affect [ə'fɛkt]
26. destroy [dɪ'strɔɪ]

27. reproduce [‚riprə'djus]
28. undergrowth ['ʌndɚ‚groθ]
29. seedling ['sidlɪŋ]
30. replace [rɪ'ples]

31. remain [rɪ'men]
32. rainfall ['ren‚fɔl]
33. process ['prɑsɛs]

almost immediately. Within a few years, a piece of barren[34] land will become a meadow. As time continues to pass, the meadow becomes a thicket. Once a few small trees sprout[35] up, the thicket is *on its way to* becoming an intermediate forest and, eventually[36], a mature forest. At each stage, the land supports[37] *a variety of* insects, spiders, birds, snakes, and other animals. By studying how forests develop, you can learn to appreciate[38] their complexity[39] and their incredible[40] ability to recover[41] from a variety of disasters[42].

Vocabulary

1. natural [ˈnætʃərəl] *adj.* related to or formed by nature, not made or changed by humans　自然的

   It is *natural* for trees to grow.

2. cycle [ˈsaɪkl̩] *n.* C a number of related events happening in a regularly repeated order　循環；週期

   The development of nature is a *cycle*.

3. development [dɪˈvɛləpmənt] *n.* C U 發展

   A parent is responsible for his child's *development*.

4. uninterrupted [ˌʌnɪntəˈrʌptɪd] *adj.* continuous　未受干擾的

34. barren [ˈbærən]
35. sprout [spraʊt]
36. eventually [ɪˈvɛntʃʊəlɪ]
37. support [səˈport]
38. appreciate [əˈpriʃɪˌet]
39. complexity [kəmˈplɛksətɪ]
40. incredible [ɪnˈkrɛdəbl̩]
41. recover [rɪˈkʌvɚ]
42. disaster [dɪzˈæstɚ]

Uncle Bill prefers to be *uninterrupted*.

5. unless [ən'lɛs] *conj.* except on the condition that 除非

   Unless he comes, the meeting will be cancelled.

6. mow [mo] *vi., vt.* to cut (grass) 割草；刈草

7. plot [plɑt] *n.* [C] a small marked or measured piece of ground for building

   or growing things 一小塊土地

8. stage [stedʒ] *n.* [C] a period of time in a process 階段

   The crimes are controlled at a very early *stage*.

9. besides [bɪ'saɪdz] *prep.* in addition to 除了⋯之外

   Besides swimming, I also love basketball.

10. prevent [prɪ'vɛnt] *vt.* to stop something happening 避免

    The fence *prevents* strangers from coming inside.

11. particular [pɚ'tɪkjələ] *adj.* unusual 特別的

    Bob is a *particular* type of man.

12. southeastern [ˌsauθ'istɚn] *adj.* of the southeast part, especially of a

    country 東南方的

13. intermediate [ˌɪntɚ'midɪɪt] *adj.* between or in the middle of two extreme

    points 中間的；中級的

    I am learning *intermediate* English.

14. mature [mə'tjur] *adj.* fully grown and developed 成熟的

    They have arrived the *mature* age.

15. broadleaf ['brɔdˌlif] *adj., n.* 闊葉（的）

16. occasionally [ə'keʒənlɪ] *adv.* sometimes 偶爾

    Occasionally he would take a walk with his wife.

17. prefer [prɪ'fɝ] *vt.* to like better 較喜歡

    I *prefer* apples to oranges.

18. manage ['mænɪdʒ] *vi., vt.* to succeed in taking, using, or doing

設法；經營

Mr. Louis knows how to *manage* his farm.

19. disrupt [dɪsˈrʌpt] *vt.* to bring or throw into disorder　分裂，瓦解

The system will be *disrupted* soon.

20. recovery [rɪˈkʌvərɪ] *n.* [U] the setting back of something　恢復；復原

People expect the *recovery* of the country.

21. despite [dɪˈspaɪt] *prep.* in spite of　儘管，不管

Despite the heavy rain, they went out.

22. attempt [əˈtɛmpt] *n.* [C] an effort made to do something　企圖

He failed in his *attempt* at rising.

23. weed [wid] *n.* [C] an unwanted wild plant, especially one which prevents crops or garden flowers from growing properly　雜草

24. wildfire [ˈwaɪldˌfaɪr] *n.* [C] a fire that spreads very quickly and uncontrollably　野火

25. affect [əˈfɛkt] *vt.* to influence　影響

26. destroy [dɪˈstrɔɪ] *vt.* to damage severely　破壞

The strong typhoon *destroyed* the roof.

27. reproduce [ˌriprəˈdjus] *vi., vt.* to produce a copy of　再生

28. undergrowth [ˈʌndəˌgroθ] *n.* [U] bushes, small trees, and other plants growing around and under trees　大樹下的灌木或矮樹

29. seedling [ˈsidlɪŋ] *n.* [C] a young plant grown from a seed　樹苗，小樹

30. replace [rɪˈples] *vt.* to change one thing for another　更換

The trees will be *replaced* by flowers.

31. remain [rɪˈmen] *vi.* to continue to be　依舊

The old man *remained* very healthy.

32. rainfall [ˈrenˌfɔl] *n.* [C][U] the amount of rain that falls in an area in a certain time　降雨，雨量

33. process [ˈprɑsɛs] *n.* ☐C☐U a procedure 過程

The *process* of making coke is not open.

34. barren [ˈbærən] *adj.* (of soil) too poor to produce a good corp （土地）不毛的；貧瘠的

The desert is a *barren* place.

35. sprout [spraʊt] *vi., vt.* to grow 發芽；成長

Coffee shops are *sprouting* up this summer.

36. eventually [ɪˈvɛntʃʊəlɪ] *adv.* in the end 最後

Eventually, the team won the game.

37. support [səˈport] *vt.* to provide the necessities of life (for people or animals) 供養；支持

We all *support* the policy.

38. appreciate [əˈpriʃɪˌet] *vt.* to understand fully 了解

We *appreciate* the complex story.

We all *appreciate*（感激）your kind help.

39. complexity [kəmˈplɛksətɪ] *n.* ☐C☐U the state of being complex 複雜；複雜性

40. incredible [ɪnˈkrɛdəbl̩] *adj.* very hard to believe 難以置信的

The news is *incredible*.

41. recover [rɪˈkʌvɚ] *vi., vt.* to return to the proper state of health, strength, ability, etc. 恢復，復原

Jean *recovered* from her cold very soon.

42. disaster [dɪzˈæstɚ] *n.* ☐C☐U a sudden serious misfortune causing great suffering and damage 災難

The earthquake has brought a *disaster* to the country.

Idioms and Phrases

1. prevent...from...　阻止…做…

    The fence *prevents* strangers *from* coming inside.

2. for example　例如

    Our friends, *for example*, Bob and Bill, have arrived.

3. keep...from...　使…無法…

    The guards are *keeping* the people *from* coming closer.

4. keep...out of...　使…不進入…

    The farmers *keep* the weeds *out of* the farm.

5. put out　滅（火）

    The firemen are *putting out* the fire.

6. open up　展開；打開

    The flowers are *opening up*.

    The butterflies *opened up* their wings.

7. make room for...　讓出空間給…

    The young usually *make room for* the old.

8. stop...from...　阻止…做…

    We can not *stop* them *from* catching the fish.

9. as long as...　只要…

    As long as we live, we have to eat.

10. on one's way to...　在某人往…的途中

    The thicket is *on its way to* becoming a forest.

    On my way to school I met my cousin.

Exercise

I True or False

(   )   1. A forest's natural cycle of growth and development will always continue.

(   )   2. Besides preventing a forest from growing, people can choose the type of forest.

(   )   3. People prevent intermediate pine forest from developing into mature broadleaf forests.

(   )   4. People prefer pine forests because pines grow faster and can be used to make products.

(   )   5. Despite human attempts to prevent broadleaf from growing, pines often manage to grow large.

(   )   6. Trying to keep broadleaf trees from growing in these forests is no trouble at all.

(   )   7. Many people feel that natural fires should not be allowed to burn.

(   )   8. The lodgepole pine is a tree that needs fire to reproduce.

(   )   9. Fire clears the undergrowth, making room for the seedlings to grow.

(   ) 10. Whether a forest is burned or cut down, it won't come back.

II Reading Comprehension

1. What will happen if people won't do anything to stop a forest's natural cycle of growth and development?

2. Besides preventing a forest from growing, what can people do?

3. How can people choose the type of forest that grows in a particular area?

4. Why do people prefer pine forests?

5. Why must these pine forests be closely managed?

6. Why do many scientists feel that natural fires should be allowed to burn?

7. What can you learn by studying how forests develop?

III Discussion

1. Do you have a front yard or backyard in your home? Do you grow anything there?

2. Have you ever mowed a lawn or pull weeds out of a garden?

3. Should we control a forest's natural cycle? Why or why not?

4. Is controlling the forest a problem in your country? Why or why not?

IV Vocabulary Selection

(   ) 1. The factory is said to have good quality _____.
    (A) control   (B) process   (C) support

(   ) 2. Due to their good research and _____, IBM have established good reputation.
    (A) development   (B) recovery   (C) particular

(   ) 3. His good explanation has _____ all my doubts.
    (A) prevented   (B) controlled   (C) removed

(   ) 4. She was _____ that she had paid the bill.
    (A) certain   (B) chosen   (C) remained

(   ) 5. The banking system will be _____ due to poor management.
    (A) managed   (B) disrupted   (C) recovered

(   )   6. _____ the heavy snow storm, the child went out for help.

     (A) Although   (B) Despite   (C) Unless

(   )   7. It is _____ that the dog saved the cat from the fire.

     (A) occasional   (B) successful   (C) incredible

(   )   8. We _____ the assistance you have given to us.

     (A) attempt   (B) appreciate   (C) continue

(   )   9. The economic _____ of the country is very fast.

     (A) recovery   (B) variety   (C) complexity

(   ) 10. They will _____ the old buildings with gun powder.

     (A) support   (B) interrupt   (C) destroy

V Word Forms

Verb	Noun	Adjective
control	control	controllable
naturalize	nature	natural
develop	development	developing
grow	growth	–
interrupt	interruption	interrupted
remove	removal	removable
prevent	prevention	preventive
manage	management	manageable
replace	replacement	replaceable
appreciate	appreciation	appreciative

1. Scientists think that birth rate is _____ (control).

2. It is _____ (nature) for men to make mistakes.

3. The economic _____ (develop) of Taiwan is a miracle.

4. The rate of population _____ (grow) of this country is about ten percent.

5. His constant _____ (interrupt) have caused much trouble.

6. The official was _____ (remove) for taking bribes.

7. _____ (prevent) is more important than cure.

8. The _____ (manage) of this company is efficient.

9. The _____ (replace) for the broken dishes were sent to you yesterday.

10. His _____ (appreciate) is shown in his eyes.

VI Idioms and Phrases

(Make any change in verb forms, if necessary.)

in recent years	put out	open up	cut down
as long as	at each stage	be used to	make room for

1. The fire engines tried to _____ the big fire.

2. The small cars have to _____ the coming of trucks.

3. _____ he has time, he will spend on learning.

4. The rope _____ save the drowning man.

5. Children's tastes differ greatly _____.

6. The flowers will _____ when the flower season sets in.

7. The farmers _____ the old trees for planting new ones.

8. _____ the stock business has been growing very fast.

VII Matching

_____ 1. A natural cycle of growth   a. scientists have begun to understand this.

_____ 2. By cutting the grass,   b. own the land prefer pine forests.

_____ 3. The people who   c. natural fires are useful.

_____ 4. Despite human attempts,   d. will continue uninterrupted.

_____ 5. In recent years,   e. you stop the forest at a very early stage.

_____ 6. Many now feel that   f. oaks manage to grow fairly large.

VIII Cloze Test

_____1_____ each stage, the land supports a _____2_____ of insects, spiders, birds, snakes, and other _____3_____. By _____4_____ how forests _____5_____, you can learn to _____6_____ their complexity and their _____7_____ ability to _____8_____ from a variety of _____9_____.

(   ) 1. (A) At   (B) On   (C) From   (D) To

(   ) 2. (A) meadow   (B) process   (C) spruce   (D) variety

(   ) 3. (A) humans   (B) animals   (C) wildfires   (D) parks

(   ) 4. (A) study   (B) studied   (C) studying   (D) to study

(   ) 5. (A) manage   (B) remain   (C) develop   (D) affect

(   ) 6. (A) attempt   (B) reproduce   (C) appreciate   (D) destroy

(   ) 7. (A) incredible   (B) certain   (C) popular   (D) intermediate

(   ) 8. (A) remain   (B) recover   (C) reproduce   (D) resist

(   ) 9. (A) controls   (B) disasters   (C) insects   (D) recoveries

Unit 3 Exercise

IX Translation

1. 最近幾年來，很多森林科學家已經開始了解在國家公園與國家森林撲滅自然野火也會影響一個地區會長出何種森林。

   In _____ years, many forest _____ have begun to _____ that _____ out natural _____ in national _____ and national _____ also _____ what type of _____ grows _____ an area.

2. 不管森林是燒掉了還是砍掉了，它都會再長出來。要阻止森林發展是很難的。

   _____ a forest is _____ or cut _____, it will _____ back. It's _____ to _____ a forest _____ developing.

X Grammar

Verb 動詞 (V.)–Tense 時態

*定義：用以表示存在、動作、狀態的字。

*時態是指用以表示時間關係的各種動詞形式。

*種類：動詞時態可分為以下十二種：

	現在	過去	未來
簡單式	I do	I did	I shall do
完成式	I have done	I had done	I shall have done
進行式	I am doing	I was doing	I shall be doing
完成進行式	I have been doing	I had been doing	I shall have been doing

Focus 3.1.1

請在 A, B, C, D 中選出一個最符合題句的正確答案。

(　) Today atomic energy _____ in medicine and industry.

　　(A) applying　(B) does it have applications

　　(C) being applied　(D) has applications

〈解析〉1. 一個句子，一定要有主詞及動詞 "S. + V."。

　　　　2. 本句能當主要動詞並使意思完整的只有 "(D)"。

〈Ans〉D

Focus 3.1.2

請在 A, B, C, D 中選出一個最符合題句的正確答案。

(　) "Bob must be very wealthy."

　　"Yes. He _____ more in one day than I do in a week."

　　(A) has been earned　(B) earns

　　(C) had earned　(D) has earnings

〈解析〉1. "do" 代替前面的動詞。

　　　　e.g. "Do you like it?" "Yes. I do." (do 代替 like)

　　　　2. 如果是完成式，則必須用 have, has, had 來代替。

　　　　e.g. He has made more money than I have.

〈Ans〉B

Focus 3.1.3

請在 A, B, C, D 中選出一個最符合題句的正確答案。

(　) In recent years, many forest scientists _____ to understand that natural wildfires are influential.

　　(A) begin　(B) have begun　(C) had begun　(D) have been begun

〈解析〉1. "in recent years"（最近幾年來）一般用現在完成式。

2. "begin" 用主動。

〈Ans〉B

Focus 3.2.1

請在 A, B, C, D 中找出一個不符合正確語法的錯誤之處。

(　) There are vineyards in California that product some of the best
　　　　　　　　　　　　　　　　　　　(A)　　(B)　　　　　　　(C)

wine in the world.
(D)

〈解析〉一個句子，一定要有主詞及動詞 "S. + V."，子句亦然。

e.g. I know the truth.

I know that he is right.

所以，子句裏 "product" 為名詞，須改為動詞 "produce"。

〈Ans〉B, product → produce

Focus 3.2.2

請在 A, B, C, D 中找出一個不符合正確語法的錯誤之處。

(　) The people who own the land prefer pine forests because pines
　　　　　　　　　(A)　　　　　(B)　　(C)

had grown faster.
(D)

〈解析〉一般事實的推論、陳述，以現在式表達即可。

e.g. The pen is mightier than the sword.

Facts speak louder than words.

〈Ans〉D, had grown → grow

Focus 3.2.3

請在 A, B, C, D 中找出一個不符合正確語法的錯誤之處。

(　) <u>As long as</u> the soil <u>has remained</u>, the process of <u>recovery</u> <u>begins</u>
   (A)   (B)   (C) (D)
almost immediately.

〈解析〉副詞子句裏以現在式代表未來。

  e.g. As long as he comes, she will be happy.

    If he comes, I will stay home.

〈Ans〉B, has remained → remains

XI Short Story

A Story from Mexico

Long, long ago the Aztec people went on a journey to find a home. They traveled from the north. They went through the land that is now the United States. The trip lasted many years. Babies were born, grew old, and died. The Aztecs kept walking. At last they came to Mexico.

The people were tired. "When can we stay in one place?" a man asked. "We want to stop and build our homes."

The priests said, "Our god Mexitla told us to go on. He told us there is a good place for us. The place is never too hot and never too cold. It's never too wet and never too dry. Mexitla will show us a sign when it's time to stop."

"What will he show us?" the people asked. "How will we know to stop?"

"We will see an eagle," the priest said. "A very large eagle, like a king among birds."

"We see many large eagles," a woman said.

The priest said, "Our god Mexitla said that the eagle will have a snake in its beak. The eagle will sit on a cactus plant and eat the snake."

The people continued their long journey. They crossed rivers and streams, and they climbed mountains. After a long time they came to a lovely place that was not too hot and not too dry.

"This is a wonderful place," they said. "Maybe the eagle is here." They waited for the eagle, but it did not come.

The priests said, "We cannot stay here. We will go on." So the people traveled on.

"I want to find the eagle soon," a woman said. She sounded very tired. Everyone agreed with her. They wanted to find the eagle, too. They kept on walking. They hoped the land of the eagle was not too far away.

At last the Aztecs came to a beautiful place. It was a small strip of land next to a pretty lake. The Toltec people who lived there were angry. They tried to drive the Aztecs away.

The Aztecs fought bravely. There were many fierce battles. At last the Aztecs won.

One evening two priests walked around the lake to look for a safe place to stay.

"There are many cactus plants near this lake," one priest said.

The other priest said, "Look! Up there!"

A large eagle flew overhead. Suddenly it dove down and picked up a snake. As the priests watched, it flew to the cactus. The eagle sat on the cactus and ate the snake.

The Aztecs had their sign! They built Mexico City at the side of the beautiful lake.

Today you can see the eagle and the snake on the flag of Mexico.

XII Poem

The Skylark

–Christina Rossetti

The earth was green, the sky was blue:
I saw and heard one sunny morn,
A skylark hang between the two,
A singing speck above the corn;

A stage below, in gay accord,
White butterflies danced on the wing,
And still the singing skylark soared,
And silent sank and soared to sing.

雲雀

—— 克莉斯汀娜‧羅瑟蒂

翠綠大地，蔚藍天空：
在陽光普照的清晨，
我見雲雀掛於天際，
傾聽牠麥田上高歌；

低飛和著雲雀節拍，
白蝴蝶展翅擺舞，
高歌雲雀仍翱翔自在，
屏息下降又昇歡歌。

Rhyme-scheme: a b a b c d c d

作者簡介：

Christina Rossetti（克莉斯汀娜‧羅瑟蒂）(1830–1894)

生於英國倫敦，父親為倫敦大學教授，從小就喜歡作詩。在十二歲，便有詩歌作

Unit 3 Exercise

品問世，不久便有長篇詩集與童謠歌集陸續出版。其作品樸實自然，深得拉斐爾前派的真諦，頗受讀者歡迎。自幼篤信英國國教，終生未嫁，靠宗教信仰和寫作過生活。「聖潔美麗」為其特色。

XIII Words Review

1. allow *v.* 允許
2. choose *v.* 選擇
3. cone *n.* 毬果
4. continue *v.* 繼續
5. control *v.* 控制
6. fairly *adv.* 公平地
7. fir *n.* 針樅
8. furniture *n.* 家具
9. growth *n.* 成長
10. hickory *n.* 山胡桃木
11. insect *n.* 昆蟲
12. lawn *n.* 草皮
13. lodgepole pine *n.* 海灘松
14. national *adj.* 國家的
15. oak *n.* 橡樹
16. pine *n.* 松樹
17. product *n.* 產品
18. pull *v.* 拉；拔
19. remove *v.* 移去，除去
20. snake *n.* 蛇
21. spider *n.* 蜘蛛
22. thicket *n.* 雜木叢
23. type *n.* 種類
24. variety *n.* 多樣性

4 Unit Four

Your Personality in the Palm of Your Hand?

heart line

mount of Upper Mars

head line

mount of moon

life line

mount of Venus

1. Do you believe in fortunetelling?
2. What is palm-reading? Do you believe it?
3. What can your palm tell you?

Throughout[1] history, people have been fascinated[2] by the mysteries[3] of the human personality[4]. In their efforts[5] to find out how and why humans differ[6] *from each other*, people have *looked for* answers in the stars, in the analysis[7] of handwriting[8] and drawings, in the study of the shape of the head, and in the lines and shapes of the hand.

Anyone can look at a human hand and deduce[9] some facts about the owner. For example, a hand with blisters[10] and calluses[11] tells us its owner does hard physical[12] labor[13], while a soft hand with long nails tells us the owner does not. But some people have *gone way*[14] *beyond* that simple step to a much more exotic[15] way of analyzing[16] a person's character[17]. Through the ages, these analysts[18] have identified[19] and studied different lines and shapes (called mounts[20]) in the palm[21] of the hand and have connected[22] them to certain human personality traits[23].

Experts[24] in palm reading identify nine separate lines in the

---

1. throughout [θruˈaʊt]
2. fascinate [ˈfæsn̩ˌet]
3. mystery [ˈmɪstərɪ]
4. personality
   [ˌpɝsn̩ˈælətɪ]
5. effort [ˈɛfɚt]
6. differ [ˈdɪfɚ]
7. analysis [əˈnæləsɪs]
8. handwriting

[ˈhændˌraɪtɪŋ]
9. deduce [dɪˈdjus]
10. blister [ˈblɪstɚ]
11. callus [ˈkæləs]
12. physical [ˈfɪzɪkl̩]
13. labor [ˈlebɚ]
14. way [we]
15. exotic [ɪgˈzɑtɪk]
16. analyze [ˈænl̩ˌaɪz]

17. character [ˈkærɪktɚ]
18. analyst [ˈænl̩ɪst]
19. identify [aɪˈdɛntəˌfaɪ]
20. mount [maʊnt]
21. palm [pɑm]
22. connect [kəˈnɛkt]
23. trait [tret]
24. expert [ˈɛkspɝt]

human palm. The length and clarity[25] of these lines determine[26] certain aspects[27] of personality. *For instance*, three of the most important lines are the life line, the head line, and the heart line. A long life line shows that the owner will *keep on* living a healthy life 20 to a very old age. The head line is related to intelligence[28]; a long, curved[29] line shows that the owner *is used to* thinking imaginatively[30]. The heart line shows love and affection[31]. A short line indicates[32] that the owner has problems expressing[33] affection; *in contrast*, a long, strong line shows that the owner enjoys having 25 passionate[34] relationships.

In addition to identifying lines, readers also look at nine mounts, rounded parts of the palm, that indicate other character traits. These mounts can be flat, round, or very developed[35]. For example, three of the important mounts are the mount of Venus, 30 the mount of the moon, and the mount of Upper Mars. A flat mount of Venus indicates poor health. If the mount of Venus is round, it shows that the owner works at having a healthy mind and body through exercise and correct eating. It also indicates a love of being with and helping other people. 35

25. clarity [ˈklærətɪ]

26. determine [dɪˈtɜmɪn]

27. aspect [ˈæspɛkt]

28. intelligence
[ɪnˈtɛlədʒəns]

29. curve [kɜv]

30. imaginatively
[ɪˈmædʒəˌnetɪvlɪ]

31. affection [əˈfɛkʃən]

32. indicate [ˈɪndəˌket]

33. express [ɪkˈsprɛs]

34. passionate [ˈpæʃənɪt]

35. developed [dɪˈvɛləpt]

The owner of a round mount of the moon loves traveling and has a sensitive[36] nature[37]. A strongly developed mount of the moon can indicate creative[38] thinking. A person with a flat mount of Upper Mars *can't help* believing what other people say; the

40   owner trusts[39] people and easily does what others suggest. A very developed mount of Upper Mars, however, indicates that the owner has difficulty in controlling angry feelings and other strong emotions[40].

    After interpreting[41] all the lines and mounts, experts in palm

45   reading say they can then describe[42] a person's personality. (Of course, people who have flat mounts of Upper Mars will believe what the palm reader says; people who have round ones probably[43] won't!)

1. throughout [θruˈaʊt] *prep.* during the whole period of 貫穿
   Throughout history, men have been trying to control nature.

2. fascinate [ˈfæsn̩ˌet] *vt.* to attract and hold the interest or attention of 迷惑
   Men are usually *fascinated* by the beauty of nature.

3. mystery [ˈmɪstərɪ] *n.* ⓒ something which can not be explained or understood 神秘難以理解的事物

36. sensitive [ˈsɛnsətɪv]   39. trust [trʌst]   42. describe [dɪˈskraɪb]
37. nature [ˈnetʃɚ]   40. emotion [ɪˈmoʃən]   43. probably [ˈprɑbəblɪ]
38. creative [krɪˈetɪv]   41. interpret [ɪnˈtɝprɪt]

They are learning the *mystery* of space.

4. personality [ˌpɚsn̩ˈælətɪ] *n.* C U the whole nature or character of a particular person 個性；人格

    He has a very strong *personality*.

5. effort [ˈɛfɚt] *n.* C U an attempt using all one's powers 努力

    Giving up smoking needs great *efforts*.

6. differ [ˈdɪfɚ] *vi.* to be unlike in nature, quality, amount, or form 相異，不同

    Tastes *differ*.

7. analysis [əˈnæləsɪs] *n.* C U work done to find facts and solutions to problems; a study 分析

    We must make a close *analysis* of the causes of the accident.

8. handwriting [ˈhændˌraɪtɪŋ] *n.* U the style or appearance of one's handwriting 筆跡

    The teacher praised him for his good *handwriting*.

9. deduce [dɪˈdjus] *vt.* to reach a decision or judgment about a fact by using one's knowledge or reason 推斷出

    If you see a doctor entering a house, you may *deduce* that someone in the house is ill.

10. blister [ˈblɪstɚ] *n.* C a thin watery swelling under the skin, caused by rubbing, burning, etc. 水泡

    If your shoes are too tight, you may get *blisters* on your feet.

11. callus [ˈkæləs] *n.* C an area of thick hard skin 硬皮，繭

12. physical [ˈfɪzɪkl̩] *adj.* of or for the body 身體的

    He is in good *physical* condition.

13. labor [ˈlebɚ] *n.* U effort or work, especially tiring physical work 勞動，勞力

The *labor* costs are rising.

14. way [we] *adv.* far   遠遠地；大大地

15. exotic [ɪgˋzɑtɪk] *adj.* from another part of the world   外來的，來自外國的

These clothes are *exotic*.

16. analyze [ˋænḷ͵aɪz] *vt.* to study   分析

The police are *analyzing* the case.

17. character [ˋkærɪktɚ] *n.* C U the combination of qualities or features that make one person different from others   性格；品格

Mr. Brown is a man of good *character*.

18. analyst [ˋænḷɪst] *n.* C one who studies and gives information about analyses   分析師

The *analyst* is talking about the stock market.

19. identify [aɪˋdɛntə͵faɪ] *vi., vt.* to discover or recognize   認出

I can't *identify* my umbrella among these.

20. mount [maʊnt] *n.* C a mountain or hill   小山

21. palm [pɑm] *n.* C the inside of the central part of the hand   手掌

22. connect [kəˋnɛkt] *vi., vt.* to relate, link   連接

The town is *connected* to the others by a railway.

23. trait [tret] *n.* C a particular quality, especially of a person; characteristic   特性，特徵

His good personality *traits* helped him get the job.

24. expert [ˋɛkspɝt] *n.* C one who has special skill or knowledge   專家

Mr. Lin is an *expert* in physics.

25. clarity [ˋklærətɪ] *n.* U clearness   明確，清晰

The *clarity* of thinking is important.

26. determine [dɪˋtɝmɪn] *vi., vt.* to form a firm intention or decision   決定，決心

We *determined* to do this at any cost.

27. aspect [ˈæspɛkt] *n.* C a particular side of a many-sided situation, idea, plan, etc. 方面

   The leader is right in this *aspect*.

28. intelligence [ɪnˈtɛlədʒəns] *n.* U ability to learn, reason, and understand 智力，智能

   His *intelligence* helped him solve the problems.

29. curve [kɝv] *vi., vt.* to bend in the shape of a curve 彎曲；使彎曲

   This is a very *curved* road.

30. imaginatively [ɪˈmædʒəˌnetɪvlɪ] *adv.* through imagination 出於想像地；富於想像力地

31. affection [əˈfɛkʃən] *n.* U gentle lasting love 愛

   Carol showed great *affection* for her children.

32. indicate [ˈɪndəˌket] *vt.* to show 表示，顯示

   Fever *indicates* sickness.

   A signpost *indicated* the right road for us to follow.

33. express [ɪkˈsprɛs] *vt.* to show 表示

   A smile *expressed* her joy at the good news.

34. passionate [ˈpæʃənɪt] *adj.* able to feel strongly with passion 熱情的

   Ann made a *passionate* speech last night.

35. developed [dɪˈvɛləpt] *adj.* advanced 發達的；成熟的

   His business is well *developed*.

   His long life line is clearly *developed*.

36. sensitive [ˈsɛnsətɪv] *adj.* strongly or easily influenced or changed by something 敏感的

   He is very *sensitive* to cold weather.

37. nature [ˈnetʃɚ] *n.* CU the qualities that make someone or something

different from others; character 性質；天性

It is his *nature* to be generous.

People love to be close to *nature*（自然）.

38. creative [krɪˋetɪv] *adj.* imaginative and inventive 有創造力的

    The boy is good at *creative* thinking.

39. trust [trʌst] *vt.* to believe 信任，相信

    We have to *trust* each other.

40. emotion [ɪˋmoʃən] *n.* C any of the strong feelings of the human spirit
    情感

    He showed his strong *emotions* in writing.

41. interpret [ɪnˋtɝprɪt] *vt.* to explain the meaning of 解釋

    The accident probably was wrongly *interpreted*.

42. describe [dɪˋskraɪb] *vt.* to give a picture of something in words
    描述；描寫

    Lucy *described* her feelings in poetry.

43. probably [ˋprɑbəblɪ] *adv.* perhaps 可能，或許

    Probably you are right.

Idioms and Phrases

1. differ from... 與…不同

   Apples *differ from* bananas in many ways.

2. each other 互相

   The two brothers learn to help *each other*.

3. look for... 尋找…

   They are *looking for* the missing dog.

4. go beyond... 超過⋯

Some people have *gone* way *beyond* basic computer skills.

5. for instance 例如

Lily loves flowers, *for instance*, rose, sunflower, etc.

6. keep on... 繼續⋯

The lady will *keep on* living happily to a very old age.

7. be used to + Ving 習慣於⋯ (= be accustomed to + Ving)

The students *are used to* thinking creatively.

8. in contrast 相比之下

Black stands for evil. *In contrast*, white shows good.

9. in addition to... 除⋯之外

In addition to physics, he also learned chemistry.

10. can not help + Ving 不禁

She *can not help crying*.

Exercise

I True or False

( ) 1. People have been fascinated by the mysteries of the human personality.

( ) 2. Anyone can look at a human hand and deduce some facts about the owner.

( ) 3. A soft hand with long nails tells us its owner does hard physical labor.

( ) 4. A hand with blisters and calluses tells us its owner is not a laborer.

( ) 5. Experts in palm reading identify nine separate lines in the human palm.

( ) 6. The length and clarity of these lines determine certain aspects of personality.

( ) 7. A long life line shows that the owner is used to thinking imaginatively.

( ) 8. A long head line shows that the owner will keep on living to a very old age.

( ) 9. A round mount of Venus indicates poor health.

( ) 10. The owner of a round mount of the moon loves traveling.

II Reading Comprehension

1. What have people throughout history been fascinated by?

2. Where have people looked for answers to see that they differ from each

other?

3. What does a hand with blisters and calluses tell us?

4. What does a soft hand with long nails tell us?

5. How many separate lines do experts in palm reading identify in the human palm?

6. What are the three most important lines?

7. What does a long life line show?

8. What is the head line related to?

 **Discussion**

1. What are the ways that people analyze personality?

2. What does the palm reading tell us?

3. Do you believe in palm reading? Why and why not?

4. In your country what are the ways of fortunetelling?

IV Vocabulary Selection

(　　) 1. I was greatly _____ by the beautiful scenery.

　　　　(A) fascinated　(B) shaped　(C) analyzed

(　　) 2. People made great _____ to keep good environments.

　　　　(A) calluses　(B) analysis　(C) efforts

(　　) 3. How he solved the problem still remains a _____.

　　　　(A) character　(B) mystery　(C) drawing

(　　) 4. The detective will _____ good answers from the traces.

　　　　(A) deduce　(B) identify　(C) connect

(　　) 5. She wore an _____ dress which she bought from Japan.

(A) indicated　(B) exotic　(C) identified

(　) 6. Jane is _____ to cold weather. She always sneezes.

(A) imaginative　(B) sensitive　(C) creative

(　) 7. Parents show great _____ for their children.

(A) creation　(B) relation　(C) affection

(　) 8. His income is very high. In _____, mine is much low.

(A) contrast　(B) length　(C) trust

(　) 9. The ladies are very _____. They welcome us warmly.

(A) imaginative　(B) intelligent　(C) passionate

(　) 10. Fever and cough _____ a bad cold.

(A) connect　(B) indicate　(C) analyze

V Word Forms

Verb	Noun	Adjective
–	mystery	mysterious
analyze	analysis	analystic
deduce	deduction	deductive
identify	identity	identical
connect	connection	connective
lengthen	length	long
certify	certainty	certain
relate	relation	related
–	passion	passionate
describe	description	descriptive

1. Allen likes to read _____ (mystery) stories.

2. The experts try to _____ (analysis) the case.

3. He introduced _____ (deduce) methods to us.

4. These two models are _____ (identify) in style.

5. The two towns are _____ by a long bridge.

6. The ship is 40 feet in _____ (long).

7. I said with _____ (certain) that I was right.

8. The club members are closely _____ (relate).

9. Abe made friends with many _____ (passion) people.

10. The beautiful scenery is beyond _____ (describe).

VI Idioms and Phrases

(Make any change in verb forms, if necessary.)

find out	differ from	each other	look for
look at	keep on	related to	be used to
in contrast	in addition to		

1. Tad is tall. _____, Don, his brother, is short.

2. _____ piano, he can also play the guitar.

3. The little boy is closely _____ me.

4. Bob waited and _____ his watch all the time.

5. Mother will _____ waiting until he comes back.

6. Trees _____ vegetables in many ways.

7. Tom _____ getting up at 5:00 in the morning.

8. They will finally _____ the truth.

9. He is _____ his lost key in the room.

10. The teacher told us that we should love _____.

VII Matching

_____ 1. Through the ages,

_____ 2. The head line is

_____ 3. Anyone can look at a human hand

_____ 4. The heart line shows

_____ 5. In addition to identifying lines,

_____ 6. The owner of a round mount of the moon

a. loves traveling.

b. readers also look at nine mounts.

c. related to intelligence.

d. analysts have identified and studied these lines.

e. and deduce some facts about the owner.

f. love and affection.

VIII Cloze Test

Anyone can look ____1____ a human hand and ____2____ some facts about the ____3____ . For ____4____ , a hand ____5____ blisters and calluses ____6____ us its owner ____7____ hard ____8____ labor, while a ____9____ hand with ____10____ nails tells us the owner does not.

( ) 1. (A) at (B) for (C) on (D) in

( ) 2. (A) describe (B) suggest (C) deduce (D) connect

( ) 3. (A) reader (B) owner (C) aspect (D) character

( ) 4. (A) experts (B) example (C) mount (D) personality

( ) 5. (A) of (B) with (C) from (D) on

( ) 6. (A) gives (B) travels (C) tells (D) analyzes

( ) 7. (A) does (B) lines (C) expresses (D) controls

( ) 8. (A) certain (B) physical (C) passionate (D) exotic

( ) 9. (A) soft (B) hard (C) developed (D) healthy

( ) 10. (A) short   (B) soft   (C) long   (D) hard

IX Translation

1. 經過好幾個世紀，這些分析家已經認出並研究出這些人類手掌上的不同線條及掌丘，並且已將此和某些人格特質產生關聯。

Through the _____ , these _____ have identified and _____ different _____ and shapes in the _____ of the hand and have _____ them to certain human personality _____ .

2. 在解釋過全部的線條及掌丘後，手相專家說這樣他們才能描述一個人的個性。

After _____ all the lines and _____ , experts _____ palm _____ say they can then _____ a person's _____ .

X Grammar

Article 冠詞

*定義：冠在名詞前面的形容詞叫冠詞。

*種類：常用的冠詞有：

定冠詞	the
不定冠詞	a, an

Focus 4.1.1

請在 A, B, C, D 中選出一個最符合題句的正確答案。

( ) "What do you want?"

" I want _____ that is on the table."

(A) the loaf of bread   (B) a bread

(C) a loaf of bread   (D) some bread

〈解析〉 1. "that is on the table" 為限定詞，所以要用定冠詞 "the"。

2. 麵包要用 a piece of （一片麵包）

　　　　　　a loaf of （一塊麵包）

3. 單個圓形的麵包叫作 "bun"，日語的麵包（讀 pan）源於此字。

e.g. I want to eat a bun.

〈Ans〉A

Focus 4.1.2

請在 A, B, C, D 中選出一個最符合題句的正確答案。

（　）Any one can look at ＿＿＿＿＿ human hand and deduce some facts about ＿＿＿＿＿ owner.

(A) a; a　(B) the; the　(C) a; the　(D) the; a

〈解析〉 1. 一隻手可為任何人之手，所以用 "a"。

2. 但看了一隻手後，即知其人，此人即已限定，所以用 "the"。

〈Ans〉C

Focus 4.1.3

請在 A, B, C, D 中選出一個最符合題句的正確答案。

（　）Experts in palm reading identify nine separate lines in ＿＿＿＿＿ human palm.

(A) a　(B) the　(C) an　(D) those

〈解析〉 1. "the ＋ 單數名詞" 可代表全體。

e.g. The dog is a faithful animal.

The post office helps us much.

2. "the human palm" 代表人類的手掌。

〈Ans〉B

Unit 4 Exercise

Focus 4.2.1

請在 A, B, C, D 中找出一個不符合正確語法的錯誤之處。

(　) Eminent physicians from all over the world came to the United
　　　　　　　　　　　(A)　　　　　　　　　　　(B)
　　States to celebrate a centennial of Einstein's birth.
　　　　　　　(C)　　(D)

〈解析〉對於某特定或已提到的人或事，非任何場合皆有的，必須用定冠詞。

　　　　　e.g. "centennial"（百年紀念）對一個人為特定的，所以必須用定

　　　　　冠詞 "the"。

　　　　句型：the...of...

　　　　　　　　　　　　　　　　　　　　　　　　　〈Ans〉D, a → the

Focus 4.2.2

請在 A, B, C, D 中找出一個不符合正確語法的錯誤之處。

(　) For instance, three of a most important lines are the life line, the
　　　(A)　　　　　　(B)　　　　　　　　　　(C) (D)
　　head line, and the heart line.

〈解析〉形容詞最高級前要加 "the"。

　　　　　e.g. He is the tallest among the children.

　　　　　　　　　　　　　　　　　　　　　　　　　〈Ans〉B, a → the

Focus 4.2.3

請在 A, B, C, D 中找出一個不符合正確語法的錯誤之處。

(　) The owner of a round mount of the moon loves traveling and has
　　　(A)　　　　(B)　　　　　　　(C)
　　the sensitive nature.
　　(D)

〈解析〉非限定的字要用不定冠詞。

e.g. She has a sweet nature.

　　He has a kindly nature.

有「月丘」的主人，具有敏感的個性。「敏感的個性」不必特別限
定。

〈Ans〉D, the → a

Festivals of New Year

For much of the world 1 January is celebrated as New Year's Day. Originally, this was the date of the Roman New Year. Although it occurs in the middle of summer in the southern hemisphere, like Christmas, this is truly a winter festival.

On New Year's Eve, 31 December, many people hold parties which last until late into the night. It is traditional to greet the new year at midnight on 31 December and celebrate the first minutes of the year in the company of friends and relatives. People may dance and sing together and drink a toast to the year ahead.

After the celebrations, it is time to make new year resolutions — these are a list of decisions about how to live in the coming year. Often people resolve to be honest and more generous in their relationships with others, or they may set themselves new aims to achieve at work or in their leisure activities. New Year's Day is the first day they must put these resolutions into practice.

In Scotland, New Year's Eve is called Hogmanay. It is celebrated with bonfires and feasts. At midnight a song called *Auld Lang Syne* is sung. This tells people to remember the past and look forward to the future. It is also believed that the first person to enter your home after midnight can bring you good luck. If this person carries the traditional gifts of bread, coal, and money then the family will not be poor, cold, or hungry in the coming year.

XII Poem

A Psalm of Life

–Henry Wadsworth Longfellow

Tell me not in mournful numbers,

Life is but an empty dream!

For the soul is dead that slumbers,

And things are not what they seem.

Life is real! Life is earnest!

And the grave is not its goal;

Dust thou are, to dust thou returnest,

Was not spoken of the soul.

生命之歌

——朗費羅

勿以悲傷詩句告訴我

「人生只空夢！」

靈魂睡著者，醉生夢死，

世事不如表面所示。

生命是真！生命是誠！

墳場非其終點；

「是塵土，必歸塵土，」

靈魂可不然。

Rhyme-scheme: a b a b c d c d

作者簡介：

Henry Wadsworth Longfellow（朗費羅）(1807–1882)

美國著名詩人，出生於美國緬因州的波特蘭市。1825 年畢業於玻得因學院

Unit 4 Exercise

(Bowdoin College)，為美國首位讚美愛與人生之詩人。他的成功源於他的自然價值觀的表現與精練敏銳的才能。他以獨特的親切與優美的寫作技巧聞名。

XIII Words Review

1. certain *adj.* 某些的；確定的
2. contrast *n.* 差別；對比
3. difficulty *n.* 困難
4. drawing *n.* 圖畫
5. feeling *n.* 感覺；感情
6. flat *adj.* 平坦的
7. healthy *adj.* 健康的
8. human *adj., n.* 人類的；人類
9. length *n.* 長度
10. line *n.* 線條，線
11. nail *n.* 指甲
12. related *adj.* 有關聯的
13. relationship *n.* 關係
14. separate *v.* 分開，分離
15. shape *n.* 形狀

5 Unit Five

The Day a Mountain Died

1. What is a volcano?
2. Is there any volcano in your country?
3. Do all volcanos erupt? Are all volcanos dangerous?

Mt. St. Helens is a volcano[1] in the state of Washington in the western United States. On May 18, 1980, it erupted[2] with the force of a nuclear bomb. *According to* scientists, there had been no volcanic[3] eruption[4] to equal[5] this one in the last

5　4,000 years. When Mt. St. Helens exploded[6], it released[7] energy[8] that was greater than the bomb that destroyed Hiroshima*, Japan, in 1945. The force was strong enough to send 100 million tons of dust into the atmosphere[9]. A force that strong *had* tremendous[10] effects[11] *on* the area around the volcano.

10　The visible[12] effects were awesome[13]. Once there had been green meadows[14] and thick forests; after the eruption, there was black volcanic rock and ash[15]. From the air, thousands of acres[16] of trees *looked like* scattered[17] matchsticks. Where there had once been clear streams and lakes, there were only bubbling[18] pools of

15　mud. Over 200 kilometers of streams and 26 lakes were destroyed. Once the mountain had stood tall; afterwards[19], most of its top and all of its north side were missing. The force of the eruption reduced the mountain from the fifth-tallest in the state

---

1. volcano [vɑl'keno]
2. erupt [ɪ'rʌpt]
3. volcanic [vɑl'kænɪk]
4. eruption [ɪ'rʌpʃən]
5. equal ['ikwəl]
6. explode [ɪk'splod]
7. release [rɪ'lis]

8. energy ['ɛnɚdʒɪ]
9. atmosphere ['ætməs,fɪr]
10. tremendous [trɪ'mɛndəs]
11. effect [ə'fɛkt]
12. visible ['vɪzəbl]

13. awesome ['ɔsəm]
14. meadow ['mɛdo]
15. ash [æʃ]
16. acre ['ekɚ]
17. scattered ['skætɚd]
18. bubble ['bʌbl]
19. afterwards

*Hiroshima（廣島），日本本州西南海岸城市，1945 年 8 月 6 日遭美國以原子彈襲擊。

to the thirtieth-tallest.

The economic[20] effects on the area were staggering[21]. The U.S.   20
Forest Service estimated[22] that hundreds of millions of dollars'
worth of timber[23] was destroyed, more than enough wood to build
200,000 houses. Businesses and homes simply disappeared[24]
under tons of rock, ash, and mud. Nearly 300 homes along the
Toutle River were badly damaged or destroyed. The port[25] of   25
Portland, sixty miles to the south, was clogged[26] with mud and
ash. Because the port was clogged, cargo ships could *neither*
load[27] *nor* unload[28] and sat helpless. Economists[29] estimated the
commercial[30] and personal damages in the billions[31] of dollars.

Finally, the effects on human life were tragic[32]. Thirty-four   30
bodies were recovered in the weeks following the eruption; twenty-
seven more people simply disappeared. Some of the sixty-one were
photographers and scientists who were there to record the
stirring[33] of the mountain. They thought that there would be a
warning before the final eruption; there was none. Other victims[34]   35
were campers[35] and workers who were deceived[36] by the

['æftɚwɚdz]

20. economic [ˌikəˈnɑmɪk]

21. stagger [ˈstægɚ]

22. estimate [ˈɛstəˌmet]

23. timber [ˈtɪmbɚ]

24. disappear [ˌdɪsəˈpɪr]

25. port [port]

26. clog [klɑg]

27. load [lod]

28. unload [ʌnˈlod]

29. economist [ɪˈkɑnəmɪst]

30. commercial [kəˈmɝ�·ʃəl]

31. billion [ˈbɪljən]

32. tragic [ˈtrædʒɪk]

33. stir [stɝ·]

34. victim [ˈvɪktɪm]

35. camper [ˈkæmpɚ]

36. deceive [dɪˈsiv]

40　apparent[37] calm of the mountain that bright, sunny spring morning. One——a crusty[38], old man who owned a little resort[39] five miles from the mountain——had refused[40] to leave. He said that he was part of the mountain and the mountain was part of him. His words *turned out to be* true; his body was never found.

45　*All in all*, it is impossible to calculate[41] the total effects of the eruption. It will take thousands of years for the geographical[42] damage to be erased[43]. The economy[44] of the area will perhaps never recover. Businesses have closed, never to reopen; the lakes and rivers, which had attracted visitors, are gone forever; the logging[45] industry has no trees to cut. Human life, of course, can never be replaced.

1. volcano [vɑl'keno] *n.* [C] 火山
   This is an extinct *volcano*.
2. erupt [ɪ'rʌpt] *vi.* to explode and pour out fire, lava, etc. （火山）爆發
   The volcano *erupted* suddenly.
3. volcanic [vɑl'kænɪk] *adj.* of, from, produced by or caused by a volcano
   火山的

37. apparent [ə'pærənt]
38. crusty ['krʌstɪ]
39. resort [rɪ'zɔrt]
40. refuse [rɪ'fjuz]
41. calculate ['kælkjə‚let]
42. geographical
　　[‚dʒiə'græfɪkl]
43. erase [ɪ'res]
44. economy [ɪ'kɑnə‚mɪ]
45. logging ['lɔgɪŋ]

There are many *volcanic* rocks on the mountain.

4. eruption [ɪ'rʌpʃən] *n.* C U the explosion of a volcano　（火山的）爆發

The force of the volcanic *eruption* is strong.

5. equal ['ikwəl] *vt.* to be the same as　與…相等

His strength *equals* mine.

6. explode [ɪk'splod] *vi., vt.* to blow up　爆炸

The building *exploded* and fell down.

7. release [rɪ'lis] *vt.* to set free　釋放，放出

The volcano exploded and *released* much energy.

The news was *released* yesterday.

They *released* the prisoners.

8. energy ['ɛnədʒɪ] *n.* C U the power which one can use in working　能源

Energy crisis was a problem.

Jack is a man of much *energy*.

9. atmosphere ['ætməs,fɪr] *n.* C the air　大氣；空氣

We live in an *atmosphere* of freedom.

The warm *atmosphere* in the theater made me feel faint.

10. tremendous [trɪ'mɛndəs] *adj.* very great in size, amount, or degree
極大的；可怕的

This is a *tremendous* wave.

11. effect [ə'fɛkt] *n.* C U a result or condition produced by a cause
影響，結果

The *effects* on human life were terrible.

12. visible ['vɪzəbḷ] *adj.* that can be seen　可見的

The ship was *visible* in the dark.

13. awesome ['ɔsəm] *adj.* very bad, terrible　可怕的

The great fire was an *awesome* sight.

14. meadow ['mɛdo] *n.* C U a field where cattle, sheep, etc. can feed 草地

15. ash [æʃ] *n.* U the soft grey powder that remains after something has been burnt 灰燼，灰

16. acre ['ekɚ] *n.* C a unit for measuring area 英畝

17. scattered ['skætɚd] *adj.* widely separated 分散的

18. bubble ['bʌbḷ] *vi.* to form, produce, or rise as bubbles 冒泡

    Because of the heat, the water is *bubbling*.

19. afterwards ['æftɚwɚdz] *adv.* after that 之後，以後

    Afterwards, he will live in the school dormitory.

20. economic [ˌikə'nɑmɪk] *adj.* of economics 經濟的

    The *economic* development of Taiwan is marvellous.

21. staggering ['stægərɪŋ] *adj.* almost unbelievable; very shocking 使人震驚的

    The child's talent for science is *staggering*.

    The drunkard *staggered* and fell on the ground.

22. estimate ['ɛstəˌmet] *vt.* to calculate 估計，評估

    They *estimated* the loss at US$500.00.

23. timber ['tɪmbɚ] *n.* U wood for building 木料，木材

24. disappear [ˌdɪsə'pɪr] *vi.* to go out of sight 不見，失蹤

    He *disappeared* without paying.

    The snow has *disappeared*.

25. port [port] *n.* C harbor 港

26. clog [klɑg] *vi., vt.* to become blocked or filled so that movement or activity is very difficult 阻礙

    The pipe was *clogged* with dirt.

    The port was *clogged* with mud.

27. load [lod] *vi., vt.* to put a load on or in a vehicle 裝載

The ship is *loading* cargo at Kobe.

28. unload [ʌnˈlod] *vi., vt.* to remove a load from something 卸貨

The cargo will be *unloaded* at London.

29. economist [ɪˈkɑnəmɪst] *n.* C a person who studies and is skilled in economics 經濟學家

30. commercial [kəˈmɝˌʃəl] *adj.* of, related to, or used in commerce 商業的

31. billion [ˈbɪljən] *n.* C one thousand million 十億

32. tragic [ˈtrædʒɪk] *adj.* very unfortunate 悲慘的；悲劇的

The movie was a *tragic* story.

33. stir [stɝ] *vi., vt.* to move in a circular motion through a liquid or mixture 攪動；移動

34. victim [ˈvɪktɪm] *n.* C someone that suffers pain, death, or harm 犧牲者

Many were the *victims* of war.

He fell a *victim* to the disease.

35. camper [ˈkæmpɚ] *n.* C a person who camps 露營者

36. deceive [dɪˈsiv] *vt.* to mislead 欺騙

He was *deceived* by his friends.

37. apparent [əˈpærənt] *adj.* evident 明顯的

It is *apparent* that he was careless.

38. crusty [ˈkrʌstɪ] *adj.* bad-tempered 壞脾氣的

39. resort [rɪˈzɔrt] *n.* C a place where people regularly go for holidays 渡假地

This is a good summer *resort* for swimming.

40. refuse [rɪˈfjuz] *vi., vt.* to say no 拒絕

He *refused* to go home with me.

41. calculate [ˈkælkjəˌlet] *vt.* to estimate 計算

He is *calculating* the total income.

He is *calculating* the expenses.

42. geographical [ˌdʒiəˈgræfɪkl̩] *adj.* of or related to geography 地理上的

43. erase [ɪˈres] *vt.* to remove 除去；擦掉

    The memory can't be *erased*.

44. economy [ɪˈkɑnəˌmɪ] *n.* C U the economic conditions of a nation, a region or a family 經濟

45. logging [ˈlɔgɪŋ] *n.* U the work or industry of cutting trees 伐木；伐木業

Idioms and Phrases

1. according to... 依據…

   According to the news report, there is a storm today.

2. have an effect on... 對…有影響

   The fire *had* strong *effects on* the area.

3. look like... 看起來像…

   The snake *looks like* a rope.

4. neither...nor... 既不…也不…

   She could *neither* talk *nor* hear.

5. turn out to be... 變成…

   His words *turned out to be* true.

   He *turned out to be* a patriot.

6. all in all 總而言之

   All in all, I am right in this matter.

Exercise

I True or False

(　　) 1. Mt. St. Helens is a volcano in the state of Ohio.

(　　) 2. On May 18, 1990 it erupted with the force of a nuclear bomb.

(　　) 3. When Mt. St. Helens exploded, it released very little energy.

(　　) 4. The force was strong enough to send 100 million tons of dust into the atmosphere.

(　　) 5. There had once been clear streams and lakes, but after this eruption there were only bubbling pools of mud.

(　　) 6. Over 200 kilometers of streams and 26 lakes were destroyed by the eruption.

(　　) 7. The economic effects caused by this eruption on the area were staggering.

(　　) 8. Finally, the effects on human life were tragic.

(　　) 9. A crusty, old man who owned a little resort near the mountain finally left and survived.

(　　) 10. All in all, it is possible to calculate the total effects of the eruption.

II Reading Comprehension

1. Where is Mt. St. Helens?

2. When did Mt. St. Helens erupt? How big was the eruption?

3. What did scientists say about the eruption?

4. Were the visible effects awesome? Give some examples.

Unit 5 Exercise

5. Were the economic effects on the area staggering? Give some examples.

6. Were the effects on human life tragic? Give some examples.

7. Is it possible to calculate the total effects of the eruption? Why or why not?

III Discussion

1. How do you feel about the eruption of Mt. St. Helens? Try to find specific details and state your opinion.

2. What is the best way to protect yourself when there is an eruption of volcano? Discuss the methods and write them down in your notebook.

3. Was the crusty, old man right in refusing to leave? Discuss and analyze the character of the old man.

IV Vocabulary Selection

(　　) 1. The bomb _____ and hurt many passengers.
   (A) maintained　(B) exploded　(C) supported

(　　) 2. The volcano _____ a great deal of energy.
   (A) destroyed　(B) affected　(C) released

(　　) 3. The port of Portland was _____ with mud and ash everywhere.
   (A) clogged　(B) equaled　(C) effected

(　　) 4. After the _____, there was black volcanic rock and ash.
   (A) eruption　(B) estimation　(C) calculation

(　　) 5. Their army was beaten and _____ on the east coast.
   (A) warned　(B) destroyed　(C) damaged

(　　) 6. The volcano _____ with no sign of warning.
   (A) erupted　(B) disappeared　(C) deceived

(   ) 7. His words _____ out to be true; his body was never found.

   (A) forced   (B) recovered   (C) turned

(   ) 8. The government _____ that the loss was about US$1,000,000.

   (A) estimated   (B) scattered   (C) reduced

(   ) 9. Businesses and farms simply _____ under tons of rock.

   (A) damaged   (B) disappeared   (C) disappointed

(   ) 10. It is _____ that the ship can tide over the storms.

   (A) apparent   (B) commercial   (C) tragic

V Word Forms

Verb	Noun	Adjective
erupt	eruption	eruptive
volcanize	volcano	volcanic
equal	equal	equal
equalize	equality	
explode	explosion	explosive
energize	energy	energetic
destroy	destruction	destructive
deceive	deception	deceptive
–	tragedy	tragic
effect	effect	effective
attract	attraction	attractive

1. The _____ (erupt) of the volcano caused great damage.

2. After the eruption, there was black _____ (volcano) rock here and there.

3. Abraham Lincoln fought for the _____ (equal) of human rights.

4. The _____ (explode) of the warehouse hurt the guards.

5. The students are very _____ (energy) in sports.

6. Some children are _____ (destroy); they like to break things.

7. Appearances are often _____ (deceive).

8. "*Romeo and Juliet*" is a _____ (tragedy) love story.

9. The law becomes _____ (effect) at midnight.

10. The charming girls are _____ (attract) to people.

VI Idioms and Phrases

(*Make any change in verb forms, if necessary.*)

according to	once	with the force of	to the south
turn out	all in all	gone forever	be clogged with

1. The volcano erupted _____ a nuclear bomb.

2. _____, the total loss is not easy to be calculated.

3. Mr. Brown was _____ a policeman when he was young.

4. The hero _____ to be the mayor of the city.

5. The good old days are _____.

6. The ditches _____ stones and mud.

7. _____ the weather report, it will be a fine day.

8. My house is here. His is lying _____ of mine.

VII Matching

_____ 1. Mt. St. Helens is a volcano   a. can never be replaced.

_____ 2. The force was strong enough   b. the area were staggering.

_____ 3. The economic effects on   c. in the state of Washington.

_____ 4. Most of its top and all of its   d. the commercial damages in the
         north side   billions of dollars.

_____ 5. Economists estimated   e. to send 100 million tons of dust
                                               into the atmosphere.
_____ 6. Human life, of course,
                                            f. were missing.

VIII Cloze Test

All in _____1_____, it is _____2_____ to calculate the total _____3_____ of the
eruption. It will _____4_____ thousands of _____5_____ for the geographical
_____6_____ to be _____7_____. The economy of the _____8_____ will perhaps
never _____9_____.

( ) 1. (A) for   (B) all   (C) out   (D) none

( ) 2. (A) impossible   (B) badly   (C) awesome   (D) worth

( ) 3. (A) effects   (B) acres   (C) energy   (D) areas

( ) 4. (A) damage   (B) recover   (C) take   (D) build

( ) 5. (A) bodies   (B) years   (C) victims   (D) records

( ) 6. (A) side   (B) forest   (C) meadow   (D) damage

( ) 7. (A) erased   (B) missed   (C) followed   (D) deceived

( ) 8. (A) timber   (B) atmosphere   (C) resort   (D) area

( ) 9. (A) calculate   (B) refuse   (C) recover   (D) reduce

IX Translation

1. 攝影師及科學家以為在最後的爆發之前會有預警，結果竟然沒有；其他的受害者還有工人和去露營的人，他們被這座山祥和的外表給騙了。

The photographers and the _____ thought there _____ be a _____ before the final _____; there was _____. Other _____ were _____ and workers who were _____ by the apparent _____ of the mountain.

2. 商業都已關閉，不會再重新開業；曾吸引訪客的湖泊及河流就此永遠消失不見；伐木業也無樹可伐。當然，人類的生活也永遠無法回復到以前的樣子。

Businesses have _____, never to _____; the lakes and _____, which had _____ visitors, are _____ forever; the _____ industry has no _____ to cut. Human life, of _____, can never be _____.

X / Grammar

Preposition 介系詞 (Prep.)

*定義：為置於名詞前面的字，用以形成介系詞片語，作為形容詞或副詞之用，以媒介句子與片語之間的關係。所以稱為介系詞，又稱前置詞，因置於名詞前面之故。

*常用之介系詞有：

	正面	反面
方向	to, on, in, into, up, for, towards	away, from, off, out, out of, down
位置	at, on, in, about, around	away, from, off, out, out of
穿越	along, across, through, throughout	
因為	for, of (because of)	

Focus 5.1.1

請在 A, B, C, D 中選出一個最符合題句的正確答案。

(   ) "Where is your home town?"

"It is about twenty miles _____ the east of Chicago."

(A) in   (B) on   (C) to   (D) by

〈解析〉to the east of... 位於…之東方

e.g. Tainan lies to the south of Taipei.

〈Ans〉C

Focus 5.1.2

請在 A, B, C, D 中選出一個最符合題句的正確答案。

(   ) The port of Portland was clogged _____ mud and ash.

(A) with   (B) of   (C) on   (D) in

〈解析〉be clogged with... 為…所阻礙

e.g. The river was clogged with sand and pebbles.

〈Ans〉A

Focus 5.1.3

請在 A, B, C, D 中選出一個最符合題句的正確答案。

(   ) "Where did Carol disappear to?"

"She went to that jewelry store _____ the street."

(A) across   (B) near   (C) by   (D) from

〈解析〉across the street 在街道的那一邊

〈Ans〉A

Unit 5 Exercise

Focus 5.2.1

請在 A, B, C, D 中找出一個不符合正確語法的錯誤之處。

(　　) The progress made in space travel for the early 1960s is
　　　　　(A)　　　(B)　　　(C)　　　　　　(D)
remarkable.

〈解析〉年代用 "in"

　　　in the early 1960s 在 1960 年代初期，即 1961, 1962, 1963, etc.

〈Ans〉D, for → in

Focus 5.2.2

請在 A, B, C, D 中找出一個不符合正確語法的錯誤之處。

(　　) John lived in New York since 1960 to 1975, but he is now living in
　　　　　　　　(A)　　　　　　(B)　　　　　　　　　　(C)　　(D)
Detroit.

〈解析〉from...to... 從…到…

　　　e.g. From 1970 to 1999 he lived in Los Angeles.

　　　He moved from Miami to San Francisco.

〈Ans〉B, since → from

Focus 5.2.3

請在 A, B, C, D 中找出一個不符合正確語法的錯誤之處。

(　　) Doctors are now familiar with many incurable diseases and will be
　　　　　　　　　　(A)　　　　　　　　　　(B)
able to detect tuberculosis or certain forms of cancer at the near
　　(C)　　　　　　　　　　　　　　　　　　　　　　(D)
future.

〈解析〉in the near future 在不久的將來

in the past 在過去

at this moment 此刻，現在

時間較長，用 "in"，如 in this year, in this season, in this month, in this week, in these days

〈Ans〉D, at → in

XI Short Story

A Brother Like That

A friend of mine named Paul received an automobile from his brother as a Christmas present. On Christmas Eve when Paul came out of his office, a street urchin was walking around the shiny new car, admiring it. "Is this your car, Mister?" he asked.

Paul nodded. "My brother gave it to me for Christmas." The boy was astounded. "You mean your brother gave it to you and it didn't cost you nothing? Boy, wish..." He hesitated.

Of course Paul knew what he was going to wish for. He was going to wish he had a brother like that. But what the lad said jarred Paul all the way down to his heels.

"I wish," the boy went on, "that I could be a brother like that."

Paul looked at the boy in astonishment, then impulsively he added, "Would you like to take a ride in my automobile?"

"Oh yes, I'd love that."

After a short ride, the boy turned and with his eyes aglow, said, "Mister, would you mind driving in front of my house?"

Paul smiled a little. He thought he knew what the lad wanted. He wanted to show his neighbors that he could ride home in a big automobile. But Paul was wrong again. "Will you stop where those two steps are?" the boy asked.

He ran up the steps. Then in a little while Paul heard him coming back, but he was not coming fast. He was carrying his little crippled brother. He sat him down on the bottom step, then sort of squeezed up against him and pointed to the car.

"There she is, Buddy, just like I told you upstairs. His brother gave it to him for Christmas and it didn't cost him a cent. And some day I'm gonna give you one just like it...then you can see for yourself all the pretty things in the Christmas windows that I've been trying to tell you about."

Paul got out and lifted the lad to the front seat of his car. The shining-eyed older brother climbed in beside him and the three of them began a memorable holiday ride.

That Christmas Eve, Paul learned what Jesus meant when he had said: "*It is more blessed to give...*"

XII Poem

Ode to a Nightingale

–John Keats

Darkling I listen; and, for many a time

I have been half in love with easeful Death,

Call'd him soft names in many a mused rhyme,

To take into the air my quiet breath;

Now more than ever seems it rich to die,

To cease upon the midnight with no pain,

While thou art pouring forth thy soul abroad

In such an ecstasy!

Still wouldst thou sing, and I have ears in vain–

To thy high requiem become a sod.

夜鶯曲

—— 濟慈

在暗中我傾聽；有好幾次

幾乎要愛上安逸的死神，

妄想用詩句低喚祂的名字，

將我平靜的呼吸溶入大氣；

現在比往常看來死是富有的，

在半夜中毫無痛苦地走了，

當你正把你的靈魂傳達出來

如此地快樂！

雖然你繼續唱歌，而我有耳朵也是枉然——

對於你的安魂曲，我已變成無知覺的草皮了。

Rhyme-scheme: a b a b c d c d

作者簡介：

John Keats（濟慈）**(1795–1821)**

Unit 5 Exercise

為英國浪漫時期之偉大詩人。

他生於倫敦，出身寒賤。父親在祖父的馬匹出租店幫忙清理馬舍，濟慈十歲時，父親由馬上摔下去世；母親後改嫁，但不久離婚。十五歲時母親死於肺病。十六歲時，任外科醫師之見習生。之後雖獲醫學執照，但最後還是放棄醫術，而成為浪漫時期的大詩人。

由於家庭背景的關係，濟慈生性敏銳。歷經各種不幸事件，心中渴望遠離現實社會，因而使他活於古代之夢想中。他追求的現實，可分兩方面：「美」與「真」——「美」代表感情的世界；「真」代表想像的世界。

濟慈的作品風格多充滿古雅典故與遠離塵世的精神，並為追求完美之美與真而努力。

XIII Words Review

1. attract *v.* 吸引
2. calm *n.* 平靜
3. cargo *n.* 貨物
4. force *n.* 力量
5. helpless *adj.* 無助的
6. industry *n.* 工業
7. matchstick *n.* 火柴棒
8. missing *adj.* 生死不明的
9. mud *n.* 泥濘
10. nearly *adv.* 將近
11. north *adj.* 北方的
12. once *adv.* 一度
13. personal *adj.* 個人的
14. photographer *n.* 攝影師
15. record *v., n.* 紀錄
16. reduce *v.* 減少
17. reopen *v.* 重新開幕
18. rock *n.* 岩石
19. simply *adv.* 輕易地
20. state *n.* 州
21. stream *n.* 溪流
22. total *adj.* 總共的
23. warning *n.* 警告
24. worth *n.* 價值

6

Unit Six

Do-It-Yourself

1. Do you like to do a do-it-yourself job?
2. What are do-it-yourself jobs people usually do?
3. Why do people like to do do-it-yourself jobs?

Many homeowners hire contractors[1] to do their household[2] repairs[3]. Professional[4] painters paint the inside of homes. Professional carpenters[5] fix steps and repair doors. Plumbers[6] fix problems with toilets and sinks. And electricians[7] repair

5 problems with light switches[8] and water heaters. However, many homeowners do these types of repairs themselves. They enjoy the work so much that many of them do their own home improvements[9], too.

There are many resources[10] available that make these kinds

10 of do-it-yourself jobs easy to do. Book stores and libraries carry many books and magazines that offer suggestions and ideas for home repairs and improvements. There are also videocassettes[11] and TV shows that give complete[12] instructions[13] for building cabinets, putting tile in bathrooms, installing[14] windows, and

15 even building additional[15] rooms to enlarge[16] a home. There are also programs that show how to wax[17] wooden floors, clean fireplaces, and paint decorative[18] designs on walls. Local colleges

1. contractor [ˈkɑntræktɚ]
2. household [ˈhaʊsˌhold]
3. repair [rɪˈpɛr]
4. professional [prəˈfɛʃənl̩]
5. carpenter [ˈkɑrpəntɚ]
6. plumber [ˈplʌmɚ]
7. electrician [ɪˌlɛkˈtrɪʃən]
8. switch [swɪtʃ]
9. improvement [ɪmˈpruvmənt]
10. resource [rɪˈsors]
11. videocassette [ˈvɪdɪokəˈsɛt]
12. complete [kəmˈplit]
13. instruction [ɪnˈstrʌkʃən]
14. install [ɪnˈstɔl]
15. additional [əˈdɪʃənl̩]
16. enlarge [ɪnˈlɑrdʒ]
17. wax [wæks]
18. decorative [ˈdɛkəˌretɪv]

and high schools offer adult education classes in the evenings and on weekends. In these classes, people can learn such things as techniques[19] for building furniture and porches, ways to *set up* a solar heating system, and procedures[20] for saving energy in the home.

When homeowners *are ready to* begin their projects[21], they can go to their neighborhood[22] hardware[23] store to find many of the tools and supplies they need. These small stores sell all kinds of tools——from hammers and saws[24] to shovels[25] and wrenches[26]. They also carry electrical[27] wire, paintbrushes, toilet parts, and many types of wallpaper and colors of house paint.

Some hardware stores are larger than the typical[28] neighborhood store. They look like warehouses and sell many things at discount prices. In addition to the merchandise[29] available at the smaller hardware stores, most of these larger stores also sell doors, windows, easy-to-assemble[30] furniture, and lumber. Some also carry large plants and trees and other big items, such as lawnmowers and children's swing sets. Customers can get a lot of help at these large stores. There are guide books on

20

25

30

35

19. technique [tɛkˈnik]
20. procedure [prəˈsidʒɚ]
21. project [ˈprɑdʒɛkt]
22. neighborhood [ˈnebɚˌhʊd]
23. hardware [ˈhɑrdˌwɛr]
24. saw [sɔ]
25. shovel [ˈʃʌvl̩]
26. wrench [rɛntʃ]
27. electrical [ɪˈlɛktrɪkl̩]
28. typical [ˈtɪpɪkl̩]
29. merchandise [ˈmɝtʃənˌdaɪz]
30. assemble [əˈsɛmbl̩]

wallpapering, housepainting, carpentry, plumbing, and electrical wiring. The employees are usually happy to offer information and suggestions.

40   With a few necessary tools, some good instructions, and a little patience, do-it-yourself homeowners can become amateur[31] electricians, plumbers, carpenters, and painters. Finishing a household repair or improvement gives them a great sense of accomplishment[32] and the satisfaction[33] of learning a new skill.

45   And since they pay for only the materials and not for the labor; do-it-yourself homeowners are happy to see how much money they can save!

1. contractor [ˈkɑntræktɚ] *n.* C one that contracts to perform work or provide supply 承包工程的人；承包商
   Ms. Brown hires *contractors* to repair her bathroom.
2. household [ˈhaʊsˌhold] *adj.* of or relating to a household 家庭的
   Mother is responsible for the *household* economy of our family.
3. repair [rɪˈpɛr] *n.* C U the act of fixing 修理
   Students are learning motorcycle *repairs*.
4. professional [prəˈfɛʃənl] *adj.* of or relating a profession 專業的；職業的
   Michael Chang is a *professional* tennis player.

31. amateur [ˈæməˌtʃʊr]   [əˈkɑmplɪʃmənt]   [ˌsætɪsˈfækʃən]
32. accomplishment   33. satisfaction

5. carpenter [ˈkɑrpəntɚ] *n.* C a worker who builds or repairs wooden structure 木工

    My grandfather was a skillful *carpenter*.

6. plumber [ˈplʌmɚ] *n.* C one who repairs, installs, and maintains piping, fittings, and fixtures involved in a building 水管工人

7. electrician [ɪˌlɛkˈtrɪʃən] *n.* C one who installs, maintains, operates, or repairs electrical equipment 電工

8. switch [swɪtʃ] *n.* C a device for making, breaking, or changing the connections in an electrical circuit （電的）開關

    Please turn off the light *switch* when you leave.

9. improvement [ɪmˈpruvmənt] *n.* C U the act or process of improving 改善；改善之處

    John has made much *improvement* in his English.

10. resource [rɪˈsors] *n.* C a useful and available means 資源；手段

    He had no other *resource* but to run away.

    Playing computer games is one of his *resources*（娛樂）.

11. videocassette [ˈvɪdɪokəˈsɛt] *n.* C a cassette containing blank or prere-corded videotape 錄影帶

    The *videocassette* will show you how to make a cake.

12. complete [kəmˈplit] *adj.* having all necessary parts, elements, or steps 完全的；完整的

    The *complete* works of Shakespeare is worth buying and reading.

13. instruction [ɪnˈstrʌkʃən] *n.* C U directions 說明；說明書

    Please read the *instruction* book before using the camera.

    This manual gives complete *instructions* for the camera.

14. install [ɪnˈstɔl] *vt.* to set up 安裝

    Carpenters know well how to *install* windows.

15. additional [əˈdɪʃənl] *adj.* another 額外的

We need an *additional* room for our newly-bought computer.

16. enlarge [ɪnˈlardʒ] *vt.* to make larger; extend 加大；擴大

My employer is planning to *enlarge* his office.

17. wax [wæks] *vt.* to treat or rub with wax 用蠟擦拭⋯

Michael bought a new car recently. I often see him wash and *wax* it.

18. decorative [ˈdɛkəˌretɪv] *adj.* ornamental 裝飾用的

Please buy some *decorative* bulbs for this Christmas tree.

19. technique [tɛkˈnik] *n.* C U skill or command in doing something 技巧

Mr. Brown is famous for his unique *techniques* of painting.

20. procedure [prəˈsidʒɚ] *n.* C U an established way of doing things
程序；過程

Make sure to follow the correct *procedure* and you'll bake a delicious
cake.

21. project [ˈpradʒɛkt] *n.* C a specific plan or design, scheme 計畫，方案

We are starting a *project* to build our new house.

22. neighborhood [ˈnebɚˌhʊd] *n.* C a place or region near 鄰近

Jack went shopping in the *neighborhood* stores.

23. hardware [ˈhardˌwɛr] *n.* U ware made of metal 五金

Father asked me to buy some *hardware* in the neighborhood store.

24. saw [sɔ] *n.* C a hand or power tool used to cut hard material 鋸子

I saw a *saw* sawing a *saw*.

25. shovel [ˈʃʌvl] *n.* C a kind of hand implement 鐵鍬

26. wrench [rɛntʃ] *n.* C a hand or power tool for holding, twisting, or turning
an object 扳手

27. electrical [ɪˈlɛktrɪkl] *adj.* 電的；電動的

28. typical [ˈtɪpɪkl] *adj.* regular 典型的

Mr. Gates is a *typical* American businessman.

29. merchandise [ˈmɝtʃənˌdaɪz] *n.* U the goods that are bought and sold in business 商品

The store's *merchandise* was badly damaged in this severe earthquake.

30. assemble [əˈsɛmbl] *vt.* to bring together 裝配；集合

The president *assembled* his employees for a meeting.

31. amateur [ˈæməˌtʃʊr] *adj.* not professional; unskillful 業餘的

Father became an *amateur* photographer after he retired from his work.

32. accomplishment [əˈkɑmplɪʃmənt] *n.* C U the act of completing something successfully 成就；完成

Edison's invention of light bulbs is a remarkable *accomplishment*.

33. satisfaction [ˌsætɪsˈfækʃən] *n.* U pleasure 滿意；喜悅

Mr. Brown felt great *satisfaction* over the success of his personal concert.

Idioms and Phrases

1. set up 裝上；建立

Father will *set up* a solar heating system at home.

2. be ready to... 準備好做⋯

When we *were ready to* leave, he came for help.

Exercise

I True or False

(　　) 1. Many homeowners hire contractors to do their household repairs.

(　　) 2. Professional plumbers paint the house.

(　　) 3. The painters fix problems with toilets.

(　　) 4. Electricians repair the light switches.

(　　) 5. Homeowners who do these types of repairs themselves don't enjoy the do-it-yourself work.

(　　) 6. Local colleges offer adult education classes at noon.

(　　) 7. They can go to the book stores for hammers and saws.

(　　) 8. The hardware stores also carry many types of wallpaper.

(　　) 9. Some larger stores sell doors and windows.

(　　) 10. Do-it-yourself homeowners will pay for the labor.

II Reading Comprehension

1. What do professional painters do?

2. What do professional carpenters do?

3. What do plumbers do?

4. What do electricians do?

5. Do many homeowners also do the types of repairs themselves?

6. What are the resources available for do-it-yourself homeowners?

7. How can do-it-yourself homeowners become amateur electricians and plumbers?

III Discussion

1. Have you ever done a do-it-yourself job?

2. Have you ever helped the class with painting the walls?

3. Discuss how to fix the problems with a light switch.
   Give specific step-by-step instructions.

4. Discuss how to change a bulb in your home.
   Give specific step-by-step instructions.

IV Vocabulary Selection

(　) 1. People use a _____ to cut grass.

　　　(A) lawnmower　(B) lumber　(C) hammer

(　) 2. A _____ is a man who can fix toilets and sinks.

　　　(A) carpenter　(B) electrician　(C) plumber

(　) 3. TV shows give complete _____ for building cabinets.

　　　(A) repairs　(B) instructions　(C) contractors

(　) 4. Many resources available will make the job _____ to do.

　　　(A) electrical　(B) easy　(C) amateur

(　) 5. Noodle is a _____ kind of food in some parts of China.

　　　(A) complete　(B) professional　(C) typical

(　) 6. _____ is always right.

　　　(A) Customer　(B) Guide　(C) Homeowner

(　) 7. Workers store their materials in a _____.

　　　(A) library　(B) warehouse　(C) porch

(　) 8. Finishing the job offers us great _____.

　　　(A) procedure　(B) satisfaction　(C) resources

Unit 6 Exercise

( ) 9. Electricians will _____ a new heating system in my home.

(A) supply (B) hire (C) install

( ) 10. Some stores _____ large plants and trees.

(A) carry (B) wax (C) build

V Word Forms

Verb	Noun	Adjective
repair	repair	repairable
profess	profession	professional
electrify	electricity	electrical
typify	type	typical
improve	improvement	improvable
suggest	suggestion	suggestive
complete	completion	complete
build	building	–
decorate	decoration	decorative
educate	education	educational

1. Uncle Jim always _____ (repair) the house by himself.

2. Mike is in a _____ (profession) basketball team.

3. Joe is a salesman of _____ (electricity) items.

4. Dr. Lee is a _____ (typify) scientist in China.

5. Lisa has _____ (improve) her English greatly.

6. The trip was made at his _____ (suggest).

7. You can find a _____ (complete) story of Abraham Lincoln in the library.

8. The contractors are _____ (build) a new temple.

9. Karen painted some _____ (decorate) designs on walls.

10. The school set up good _____ (educate) programs.

VI Idioms and Phrases

(*Make any change in verb forms, if necessary.*)

on weekends	at discount prices	pay for
be ready to	type of	in addition to
most of	look like	a little
set up		

1. _____ learning is a dangerous thing.

2. The department stores are selling goods _____.

3. The thief will _____ all the troubles.

4. The carpenter does _____ his job in the town.

5. People will _____ more schools for children.

6. Cathy can speak English _____ Japanese.

7. When they _____ leave, it rained.

8. Michael is the _____ singer I admire.

9. They are planning to go on a picnic _____.

10. They _____ rich businessmen from Hong Kong.

VII Matching

_____ 1. Many homeowners hire

_____ 2. They are trying to enlarge

a. larger than the typical neighborhood store.

their home

_____ 3. Do-it-yourself homeowners are happy

_____ 4. Some stores here are

_____ 5. When they are ready to begin their projects,

_____ 6. They pay for only the materials

b. and not for the labor.

c. by building additional rooms.

d. they can go to a hardware store to find what they need.

e. to see how much money they can save.

f. contractors to help them.

VIII Cloze Test

With _____1_____ necessary tools, some good _____2_____, and _____3_____ patience, do-it-yourself homeowners can become _____4_____ electricians and painters. _____5_____ a household repair or _____6_____ gives them a great sense of _____7_____.

( ) 1. (A) a few　(B) a little　(C) few　(D) little
( ) 2. (A) cabinets　(B) plumbers　(C) paints　(D) instructions
( ) 3. (A) a few　(B) a little　(C) few　(D) little
( ) 4. (A) amateur　(B) additional　(C) decorative　(D) adult
( ) 5. (A) Finished　(B) Finish　(C) Finishing　(D) To finished
( ) 6. (A) suggestion　(B) improvement　(C) swing　(D) design
( ) 7. (A) instruction　(B) profession　(C) merchandise　(D) accomplishment

IX Translation

1. 除了在較小的五金行可買到的商品外，大部分這些較大商店也賣門、窗子、易組的家具及木材。

In _____ to the merchandise _____ at the smaller _____
stores, _____ of these larger _____ also sell doors, _____,
easy-to-assemble _____, and _____.

2. 因為他們只付材料費，不必付工資，自己動手的家庭主人會高興看到他們能
節省那麼多錢！

Since they _____ for only the _____ and not for the _____,
do-it-yourself _____ are _____ to see how _____ money
they can _____!

 Grammar

Noun 名詞 (N.)

*定義：名詞是人、動物、事物、地方等的名稱。

*種類：通常分類如下：

可數名詞	普通名詞	boy, girl, desk, etc.
	集合名詞	family, people, fish, etc.
不可數名詞	專有名詞	China, Jack, Japan, etc.
	物質名詞	water, air, iron, etc.
	抽象名詞	health, duty, wealth, etc.

Focus 6.1.1

請在 A, B, C, D 中選出一個最符合題句的正確答案。

(　) Many homeowners hire contractors to do _____.

　　(A) their household's repairs　　(B) household's their repairs

　　(C) their household repairs　　(D) repairs their household

〈解析〉1. 所有格＋名詞片語

Unit 6 Exercise

2. 非人稱不能用所有格 "'s"

例外：用於擬人稱化

e.g. A forest's natural cycle will continue.

= The natural cycle of a forest....

〈Ans〉C

Focus 6.1.2

請在 A, B, C, D 中選出一個最符合題句的正確答案。

( ) Many homeowners do these _____ themselves.

(A) types of repairs   (B) repairs of types

(C) type of repairs   (D) repair of types

〈解析〉1. 片語：a piece of, a type of

     2. these 為複數，必須接複數名詞。

〈Ans〉A

Focus 6.1.3

請在 A, B, C, D 中選出一個最符合題句的正確答案。

( ) When homeowners are ready to begin their projects, they can go to their _____.

(A) neighborhood hardware store

(B) neighborhood hardware's store

(C) hardware neighborhood store

(D) neighborhood's hardware store

〈解析〉1. 地區＋物質名詞＋主名詞

     e.g. community department store, branch toy shop

     2. 非人稱不能用所有格 "'s"

〈Ans〉A

Focus 6.2.1

請在 A, B, C, D 中找出一個不符合正確語法的錯誤之處。

(　　) There are many <u>resources</u> available that make these <u>kind</u> of <u>do-it-</u>
　　　　　　　　　　(A)　　　　　　　　　　　　　　(B)　　　(C)
<u>yourself</u> jobs easy to do.
(D)

〈解析〉these 為複數，必須接複數名詞。

〈Ans〉B, kind → kinds

Focus 6.2.2

請在 A, B, C, D 中找出一個不符合正確語法的錯誤之處。

(　　) Some <u>hardwares</u> <u>stores</u> are larger <u>than</u> the typical neighborhood
　　　　　　　(A)　　　　(B)　　　　　　(C)
<u>store</u>.
(D)

〈解析〉1. 集合名詞已含整體，複數形不能加 "s"。

　　　　如：software, footwear, information, furniture, merchandise,
　　　　etc.

　　　2. 名詞片語＝名詞＋名詞

　　　　前面的名詞具有形容詞意味，不能加 "s"。

　　　　如：boy student, office boy, etc.

　　　　複數時，"s" 要加在後面的名詞。

　　　　如：boy students, office boys

〈Ans〉A, hardwares → hardware

Unit 6 Exercise

Focus 6.2.3

請在 A, B, C, D 中找出一個不符合正確語法的錯誤之處。

(　) They look like warehouse and sell many things at discount prices.
　　　　　　　　　 (A)　　　　　　　 (B)　 (C)　　　　　 (D)

〈解析〉普通名詞要加冠詞，不然要用複數。

　　　e.g.　I am a boy.

　　　　　　We are students.

〈Ans〉A, warehouse → warehouses

 XI Short Story

Chinese New Year Customs

One week before the New Year begins, the family gathers for a ceremony in honor of the god of the kitchen. This god is believed to journey to the Emperor of Heaven and report on the family's thoughts and actions over the past year. A picture of the kitchen-god is burnt. This allows the god to leave the house, but first, the lips are smeared with honey so that only good things about the family will be told. Some families keep statues of the god, whose lips may also be smeared with honey.

On the evening before New Year, the kitchen-god is welcomed back into the home with a feast and fireworks. At New Year people eat only vegetarian meals which contain no meat. This is because each year is named after an animal. One special food is Jiaozi, dumplings made with sweetened flour which have money, gifts, or messages of good luck inside. Some of the food is set out for the spirits of dead ancestors to eat, so that they too will have a happy New Year. Children are given gifts of money, and people try to pay back any debts before the new year starts.

On New Year's Day the festival moves into the streets. Usually, an enormous paper dragon, moved by many men inside its body, dances through the streets to the music of drums. Over the doorways of houses and shops hang parcels of money which the dancers collect. This money is used to help the community and good fortune is brought to those whose money is accepted. As evening falls there may be firework displays before people return home to honor their family gods once more.

XII Poem

The Daffodils
–William Wordsworth
I wandered lonely as a cloud
That floats on high o'er vales and hills,
When all at once I saw a crowd,
A host of golden daffodils,
Beside the lake, beneath the trees
Fluttering and dancing in the breeze.

水仙花
—— 華茲華斯
我獨自漫遊　像一片浮雲
高高飄過幽谷與山丘，
突然我瞄到，
一叢金黃水仙花，
在湖旁，在樹下
在微風中　婆娑起舞。

Rhyme-scheme: a b a b c c

作者簡介：

William Wordsworth（華茲華斯）
(1770–1850)
英國的偉大田園詩人，也是浪漫派時期
詩壇的重要詩人。華茲華斯生於英格蘭
西北部風景幽美的坎伯蘭郡柯克茅斯
鎮。幼時在當地湖泊名勝區受過教育，
那裏風光明媚，使他從小就投入大自然
的懷抱，培養出最誠摯的情感。

XIII Words Review

1. available *adj.* 可利用的
2. build *v.* 建造；建築
3. cabinet *n.* 櫥櫃；檔案櫃
4. carry *v.* 備有；經營
5. customer *n.* 顧客
6. do-it-yourself *adj.* 自己動手的
7. education *n.* 教育
8. employee *n.* 雇員
9. energy *n.* 能源
10. fireplaces *n.* 壁爐
11. fix *v.* 修理
12. furniture *n.* 家具
13. guide *v., n.* 引導，指引
14. hammer *n.* 鐵槌
15. heater *n.* 暖氣機
16. hire *v.* 雇用
17. homeowner *n.* 家庭主人
18. housepaint *n., v.* 油漆
19. item *n.* 項目
20. lawnmower *n.* 除草機，割草機
21. local *adj.* 本地的，當地的
22. lumber *n.* 木材
23. necessary *adj.* 必須的
24. offer *v., n.* 提供
25. paint *v., n.* 漆；繪畫
26. paintbrush *n.* 油漆刷
27. painter *n.* 油漆匠；畫家
28. patience *n.* 耐心
29. plumb *v.* 裝水管
30. porch *n.* 走廊
31. save *v.* 節省
32. sense *n.* 感覺
33. sink *n.* 溝渠；污水槽
34. skill *n.* 技巧
35. solar *adj.* 太陽的
36. step *v., n.* 踩；樓梯
37. suggestion *n.* 建議
38. supply *v., n.* 供給
39. swing *n.* 鞦韆
40. system *n.* 系統，制度
41. tile *n.* 瓷磚，瓦
42. toilet *n.* 盥洗室，廁所
43. wallpaper *n., v.* 壁紙，貼壁紙
44. warehouse *n.* 倉庫
45. wire *n.* 電線

7 Unit Seven

Culture Shock

1. What is culture shock?
2. When do people have culture shock?
3. What should people do if they have culture shock?

"**Y**ou're going to the United States to live? How wonderful! You're really lucky!"

Does this sound familiar? Perhaps your family and friends said similar things to you when you left home. But does it seem true *all the time*? Is your life in this new country always wonderful and exciting? Specialists[1] in counseling[2] and intercultural[3] studies say that it is not easy to adjust[4] to life in a new culture[5]. They call the feelings that people experience[6] when they come to a new environment culture shock[7].

According to these specialists, there are three stages of culture shock. In the first stage, the newcomers[8] like their environment. Then, when the newness[9] *wears off*, they begin to hate the city, the country, the people, the apartment, and everything else in the new culture. In the final stage of culture shock, the newcomers begin to adjust to their surroundings[10] and, *as a result*, enjoy their life more.

Some of the reasons for culture shock are obvious[11]. Maybe the weather is unpleasant. Perhaps the customs are different. Perhaps the public service systems *such as* the telephone, post

1. specialist ['spɛʃəlɪst]
2. counseling ['kaʊnslɪŋ]
3. intercultural [ˌɪntəˈkʌltʃərəl]
4. adjust [əˈdʒʌst]
5. culture ['kʌltʃə]
6. experience [ɪkˈspɪrɪəns]
7. shock [ʃɑk]
8. newcomer ['njuˌkʌmə]
9. newness ['njunɪs]
10. surrounding [səˈraʊndɪŋ]
11. obvious ['ɑbvɪəs]

office, or transportation[12] are difficult to *figure out*, and you make   20

mistakes. The simplest things seem difficult. The language may be

difficult. How many times have you just repeated[13] the same thing

again and again and hoped to understand the answer eventually?

The food may seem strange to you, and you may miss the familiar

smells of the food you are accustomed[14] to in your own country. If   25

you don't look similar to the natives[15], you may feel strange. You

may *feel like* everyone is watching you. In fact, you are always

watching yourself. You are self-conscious[16].

　　Who experiences culture shock? Everyone does in some form

or another. But culture shock comes as a surprise to most people.   30

A lot of the time, the people with the worst culture shock are the

people who never had any difficulties in their own countries. They

were active[17] and successful in their community[18]. They had

hobbies or pastimes[19] that they enjoyed. When they come to a

new country, they do not have the same established[20] positions[21]   35

or hobbies. They find themselves without a role, almost without

an identity[22]. They have to build a new self-image[23].

12. transportation
　[ˌtrænspɚˈteʃən]
13. repeat [rɪˈpit]
14. accustom [əˈkʌstəm]
15. native [ˈnetɪv]
16. self-conscious

[ˈsɛlfˈkɑnʃəs]
17. active [ˈæktɪv]
18. community
　[kəˈmjunətɪ]
19. pastime [ˈpæsˌtaɪm]
20. established

[əˈstæblɪʃt]
21. position [pəˈzɪʃən]
22. identity [aɪˈdɛntətɪ]
23. self-image
　[ˌsɛlfˈɪmɪdʒ]

Culture shock produces a feeling of disorientation[24]. This disorientation may be homesickness[25], imagined illness, or even
40　paranoia[26] (unreasonable fear). When people feel the disorientation of culture shock, they sometimes feel like staying inside all the time. They want to protect themselves from the unfamiliar environment. They want to create an escape[27] within their room or apartment to give themselves a sense of security[28]. This escape
45　does solve the problem of culture shock for the short term, but it does nothing to familiarize[29] the person more with the culture. Familiarity[30] and experience are the long-term solutions[31] to the problem of culture shock.

Vocabulary

1. specialist [ˈspɛʃəlɪst] *n.* C a person who has special interests or skills in a limited field of work or study　專家
   Professor Li is a *specialist* in Roman history.
2. counseling [ˈkaʊnslɪŋ] *n.* U professional guidance　諮詢；建言
   The school offers *counseling* services.
3. intercultural [ˌɪntɚˈkʌltʃərəl] *adj.* between different cultures

24. disorientation
    [dɪsˌɔrɪənˈteʃən]
25. homesickness
    [ˈhomˌsɪknɪs]
26. paranoia
    [ˌpærəˈnɔɪə]
27. escape [əˈskep]
28. security [sɪˈkjʊrətɪ]
29. familiarize
    [fəˈmɪljəˌraɪz]
30. familiarity
    [fəˌmɪlɪˈærətɪ]
31. solution [səˈluʃən]

不同文化間的

Intercultural differences will be problems for most immigrants.

4. adjust [əˈdʒʌst] *vi., vt.* to change slightly to make suitable for a particular purpose 適應

It is not easy to *adjust* to life in a new culture.

5. culture [ˈkʌltʃɚ] *n.* C U the customs, beliefs, art, music and all the other products of human thought made by a particular group of people at a particular time 文化

Greek *culture* plays an important role in human history.

6. experience [ɪkˈspɪrɪəns] *vt.* to learn by experience 體驗

They *experienced* culture shock.

7. shock [ʃɑk] *n.* C U the state or feeling caused by a sudden or unexpected event 衝擊；打擊

Her father's sudden death was a great *shock* to her.

8. newcomer [ˈnjuˌkʌmɚ] *n.* C one recently arrived 新來的人

He is a *newcomer* to New York.

9. newness [ˈnjunɪs] *n.* U the sense of feeling new 新穎

When the *newness* dies, the girl won't like her teddy bear anymore.

10. surrounding [səˈraʊndɪŋ] *n.* environment 環境；周遭 (surroundings)

That little boy found himself in totally strange *surroundings*.

11. obvious [ˈɑbvɪəs] *adj.* evident 顯而易見的

It is *obvious* that we will win.

12. transportation [ˌtrænspɚˈteʃən] *n.* U means of travel from one place to another 交通

The *transportation* systems are very good in Tokyo.

13. repeat [rɪˈpit] *vi., vt.* to make, do, or perform again 重複

History will *repeat* itself.

14. accustom [əˈkʌstəm] *vt.* to make familiar with something　使習慣

I am *accustomed* to life in Japan.

15. native [ˈnetɪv] *n.* C an original inhabitant　本地人；原住民

Matthew is a *native* of Australia.

16. self-conscious [ˈsɛlfˈkɑnʃəs] *adj.* aware of oneself as an individual　自我意識的；自知的

I'm too *self-conscious* to be a good actor.

17. active [ˈæktɪv] *adj.* busy　活躍的

John is an *active* student in my class.

18. community [kəˈmjunətɪ] *n.* C a group of people having common interests　集團；社團

Will you join our artists' *community*?

19. pastime [ˈpæsˌtaɪm] *n.* C recreation, hobby　消遣

Driving is a good holiday *pastime*.

20. established [əˈstæblɪʃt] *adj.* being set up　已確立的

An *established* custom is not easy to change.

21. position [pəˈzɪʃən] *n.* C U social standing or status　社會地位，身分

Jack has won established *position* here.

22. identity [aɪˈdɛntətɪ] *n.* C U who or what a particular person or thing is　身分

Mark has become a man of great *identity*.

23. self-image [ˌsɛlfˈɪmɪdʒ] *n.* C the image of oneself　自我形象

I have been lost and can't find my *self-image* for a long time.

24. disorientation [dɪsˌɔrɪənˈteʃən] *n.* U the loss of the sense of direction　失去方向

A feeling of *disorientation* rises in my mind.

25. homesickness [ˈhomˌsɪknɪs] *n.* U longing for home and family while

absent from them 思鄉，鄉愁

He suffered from *homesickness* while he was abroad.

26. paranoia [ˌpærəˈnɔɪə] *n.* [U] a kind of psychosises 妄想症，偏執狂

27. escape [əˈskep] *n.* [C] a means of escaping 逃避的方法

Everyone wants to find an *escape* from reality.

28. security [sɪˈkjʊrətɪ] *n.* [U] safety 安全

Friendship offers a sense of *security*.

29. familiarize [fəˈmɪljəˌraɪz] *vt.* to make known or familiar 使熟悉

The guide book will *familiarize* strangers with the town.

30. familiarity [fəˌmɪlɪˈærətɪ] *n.* [U] the quality or state of being familiar 熟悉

His *familiarity* with the town will help the tourists a lot.

31. solution [səˈluʃən] *n.* [C][U] key 解決方法；解答

Please find a *solution* to this trouble.

Idioms and Phrases

1. all the time 一直，總是

The bees are busy *all the time*.

2. wear off 消滅；去除

My headache will *wear off* after one hour or two.

3. as a result 結果

The plan worked well and, *as a result*, we won the game.

He spent easily and, *as a result*, is now in debt.

4. such as... 譬如…

I like to eat fruits *such as* apples and oranges.

5. figure out 理解；算出

I can't *figure out* what he wants.

He can *figure out* the amount at once.

6. again and again 一再

John practices English *again and again*.

7. feel like... 想要…；感覺像…

I *feel like* people are watching me.

Exercise

I True or False

( ) 1. Specialists say that it is easy to adjust to life in a new culture.

( ) 2. According to this article, there are two stages of culture shock.

( ) 3. In the first stage, the newcomers like their environment.

( ) 4. When the newness wears off, they begin to love the city, the country, and the people.

( ) 5. In the final stage, the newcomers begin to adjust to their surroundings.

( ) 6. Some of the reasons for culture shock are obvious.

( ) 7. If you don't look similar to the natives, you may feel strange.

( ) 8. Very few people experience culture shock.

( ) 9. Culture shock comes as a surprise to most people.

( ) 10. Culture shock produces a feeling of disorientation.

II Reading Comprehension

1. How do the specialists call culture shock?

2. Do the specialists say that it is easy to adjust to life in a new culture?

3. According to specialists, what are the three stages of culture shock?

4. What are the reasons of culture shock?

5. What are the long-term solutions to the problem of culture shock?

III Discussion

1. Does everyone experience culture shock?

2. Have you ever experienced culture shock before?

3. Suppose one day if you go to America, what kind of culture shock will you experience?

4. Is staying inside the best solution to the problem of culture shock? Why and why not? (Discuss the good points and bad points of staying inside.)

IV Vocabulary Selection

( ) 1. A scientist is quite _____ with science.
   (A) similar   (B) familiar   (C) obvious

( ) 2. It is natural for men to make _____.
   (A) environments   (B) experiences   (C) mistakes

( ) 3. History will _____ itself.
   (A) adjust   (B) accustom   (C) repeat

( ) 4. I am quite _____ to life in Australia.
   (A) accustomed   (B) sounded   (C) escaped

( ) 5. The handbook will _____ the tourists with cultures.
   (A) familiarize   (B) imagine   (C) identify

( ) 6. The police will _____ the people from being hurt.
   (A) produce   (B) protect   (C) escape

( ) 7. Dr. Wang has won _____ position in the society.
   (A) created   (B) surprised   (C) established

( ) 8. Home always offers a sense of _____.

(A) paranoia   (B) security   (C) self-image

(　)　9. Mark Twain was a writer. He liked to _____ something.

(A) solve   (B) create   (C) result

(　) 10. His only _____ is playing golf.

(A) pastime   (B) identity   (C) disorientation

V Word Forms

Verb	Noun	Adjective
familiarize	familiarity	familiar
–	similarity	similar
excite	excitement	exciting
specialize	specialty	special
	specialist	
adjust	adjustment	adjustable
hate	hatred	–
repeat	repetition	repetitious
surprise	surprise	surprising
succeed	success	successful
solve	solution	–

1. _____ (familiar) breeds contempt.

2. This model is _____ (similarity) to that one.

3. Readers love to read _____ (excite) stories.

4. Dr. Chen is a _____ (special) in counseling.

5. Bill _____ (adjustment) his glasses and smiled.

6. Strong love will cause strong _____ (hate).

7. The bird will _____ (repetition) the word.

8. This is a _____ (surprise) news to us.

9. All people hope to _____ (success) soon.

10. This is a good _____ (solve) to the cultural problem.

VI Idioms and Phrases

(*Make any change in verb forms, if necessary.*)

according to	wear off	as a result	figure out
make mistakes	feel like	in fact	again and again

1. _____, they were very kind to the old man.

2. Men should not be afraid to _____.

3. When I am on an airplane, I _____ a bird.

4. He spoke so fast that I could not _____ what he said.

5. The doctor told me that my pains would _____ soon.

6. His ears were not good. I repeated the words _____.

7. Bob was too careless. _____, he lost his wallet.

8. _____ the radio, a strong typhoon is coming.

VII Matching

_____ 1. Your family and friends said   a. as a surprise to people.

_____ 2. Culture shock comes   b. without a role.

_____ 3. They had hobbies   c. the same established positions.

_____ 4. They do not have   d. that they enjoyed.

_____ 5. This escape does solve   e. similar things to you.

_____ 6. They found themselves   f. the problem of culture shock.

VIII Cloze Test

Culture shock _____1_____ a feeling of _____2_____. This disorientation may be _____3_____, _____4_____ illness, or _____5_____ paranois. _____6_____ people feel the disorientation of _____7_____ shock, they sometimes feel like _____8_____ inside all the time. They want to protect themselves _____9_____ the _____10_____ environment.

(　　) 1. (A) produces　(B) escapes　(C) imagines　(D) excites
(　　) 2. (A) self-image　(B) mistake　(C) environment　(D) disorientation
(　　) 3. (A) home　(B) homeless　(C) homesick　(D) homesickness
(　　) 4. (A) imagined　(B) smelled　(C) hated　(D) created
(　　) 5. (A) ever　(B) even　(C) more　(D) so
(　　) 6. (A) What　(B) How　(C) When　(D) Since
(　　) 7. (A) culture　(B) food　(C) simple　(D) language
(　　) 8. (A) crying　(B) staying　(C) wearing　(D) adjusting
(　　) 9. (A) of　(B) from　(C) to　(D) for
(　　) 10. (A) active　(B) secure　(C) final　(D) unfamiliar

IX Translation

1. 很多時候，遭受文化衝擊最嚴重的人是那些在本國從來沒有遇過困難的人。

   A _____ of the time, the _____ with the worst culture shock _____ the people _____ never had any _____ in their _____ countries.

2. 這樣逃避確能短期解決文化衝擊的問題，但無助於使此人更了解文化，熟悉

Unit 7 Exercise

與經驗才能長期解決文化衝擊的問題。

This escape does _____ the problem of _____ shock for the _____ term, but it does _____ to _____ the person more _____ the culture. _____ and _____ are the long-term _____ to the _____ of culture shock.

Grammar

Adjective 形容詞 (Adj.)

*定義：形容詞為修飾名詞或代名詞的字。

*種類：常用的形容詞種類如下：

性狀形容詞	good, nice, young, tall, etc.
代名形容詞	this, each, every, my, who, etc.
數量形容詞	much, many, few, little, all, etc.

Focus 7.1.1

請在 A, B, C, D 中選出一個最符合題句的正確答案。

( ) "Do you like the Chinese food served in American restaurants?"

"It's not bad but I prefer _____."

(A) Chinese food authentically   (B) Chinese authentic food

(C) food Chinese authentically   (D) authentic Chinese food

〈解析〉1. 性狀形容詞＋國名＋名詞

　　　　　e.g. good Chinese food, a nice English girl

　　　　2. authentic（真正的；可靠的）為性狀形容詞。

〈Ans〉D

Focus 7.1.2

請在 A, B, C, D 中選出一個最符合題句的正確答案。

(　) Some of the reasons for culture shock are _____.

(A) obvious　(B) obviously　(C) to be obvious　(D) as obvious

〈解析〉1. be 動詞後要接形容詞。

2. 另外 be 動詞亦可接：

(1) Ving　　現在分詞　I am singing.

(2) V.p.p.　　過去分詞　I am tired.

(3) Infinitive　不定詞　To see is to believe.

(4) N.　　　名詞　I am a student.

〈Ans〉A

Focus 7.1.3

請在 A, B, C, D 中選出一個最符合題句的正確答案。

(　) The simplest things seem _____.

(A) difficult　(B) be difficultly

(C) difficulty　(D) be difficult

〈解析〉1. "seem" 為連綴動詞，故後要接形容詞。

2. 一般動詞後要接副詞。

e.g. He ran quickly.

We did it carefully.

3. 只有連綴動詞（含感官動詞）後要接形容詞：

連綴動詞：be, keep, lie, stand, become, grow, get, turn, make

感官動詞：feel, sound, taste, smell, appear, seem, look

e.g. He keeps happy.

It sounds good.

〈Ans〉A

Focus 7.2.1

請在 A, B, C, D 中找出一個不符合正確語法的錯誤之處。

(　　) The average age of the Mediterranean olive trees grow today is
　　　　　　(A)　　　　　　(B)　　　　　　　(C)

two hundred years.
　　(D)

〈解析〉一個句子如無連接詞，不能有兩個主要動詞。

1. 主要動詞為 "is"，因不能有兩個動詞，所以 "grow" 必須為現在分詞或過去分詞。因 "trees" 之種植屬於被動，所以改為 "grown"。

2. 原來句法為：

The average age of the Mediterranean olive trees which are grown today is....

〈Ans〉C, grow → grown

Focus 7.2.2

請在 A, B, C, D 中找出一個不符合正確語法的錯誤之處。

(　　) Is your life in this new country always wonderful and excited?
　　　　(A)　　　　(B)　　　　(C)　　　(D)

〈解析〉1. 現在分詞與過去分詞的用法

現在分詞 (Ving)：用於主動

e.g. I saw a boy singing there.

過去分詞 (V. p.p.)：用於被動

e.g. I saw a broken window.

2. 情慾動詞：如 please, anger, surprise, astonish, shock, excite, interest, etc.

人（被動）：I am pleased to see you.

He was excited to meet me.

We are interested in English.

物（主動）：The story is interesting.

The news is surprising.

The life is exciting.

〈Ans〉D, excited → exciting

Focus 7.2.3

請在 A, B, C, D 中找出一個不符合正確語法的錯誤之處。

(　) When they <u>come to</u> <u>a new country</u>, they do not have <u>the same</u>
     (A)   (B)   (C)
<u>establishing positions</u> or hobbies.
  (D)

〈解析〉過去分詞可當形容詞用，有被動之意味。

1. established（被動）　已建立的；穩定的

establishing（主動）　正在建立的

2. 這裏的 positions（地位）應為「被建立的」。

〈Ans〉D, establishing → established

 **XI** Short Story

Christmas Traditions

The ways of celebrating Christmas have changed little since it replaced Saturnalia. From Saturnalia came the traditions of feasting, giving parties and decorating homes with evergreen plants such as holly and ivy——a reminder that even at midwinter the powers of nature survived. When Christianity came to northern Europe, the missionaries found that the Celts and other local tribes

Unit 7 Exercise

also honored the evergreens at the winter solstice. Mistletoe was a sacred plant to the Druids of Britain and, although it was never used as an official part of Christian celebrations, at Christmas many British people still pin a sprig of mistletoe over a fireplace or at the entrance to the home.

Other Christmas customs have come from northern Europe. Some ancient peoples believed that at the winter solstice the god Odin visited earth to reward good and punish evil. As Christianity spread, St Nicholas replaced Odin in the solstice legends, bringing gifts at Christmas to good children. In the Netherlands there is still a festival of St Nicholas on 6 December. The name Santa Claus has developed from the Dutch name for St Nicholas——Sinterklaas.

At Christmas, families come together to eat on Christmas Day. Many Christians go to church on Christmas Eve for a special ceremony at midnight to welcome the day when Christ was born. Relatives and friends give presents, and on Christmas morning, children wake eagerly to see if Santa Claus has left them a special gift.

In countries with warm climate, Christmas is also a time for public celebrations. In Australia there are huge parades with marching bands. In Bombay and Goa in India there are midnight services held outdoors.

XII Poem

Flow Gently, Sweet Afton

−Robert Burns

(1)

Flow gently, sweet Afton! amang thy green braes,

Flow gently, I'll sing thee a song in thy praise;

My Mary's asleep by thy murmuring stream,

Flow gently, sweet Afton, disturb not her dream.

阿頓河

——羅伯・伯恩斯

(1)

阿頓河，慢慢流，兩岸綠油油。

風景好，水聲幽，好像催眠曲。

我瑪利，已睡熟，妙境夢裏遊。

烏雲髮，芙蓉臉，時有笑容浮。

Rhyme-scheme: a a b b

(2)

Thou stockdove whose echo resounds thro' the glen,

Ye wild whistling blackbirds in yon thorny den,

Thou green-crested lapwing, thy screaming forbear,

I charge you, disturb not my slumbering Fair.

(2)

野白鴿，別咕咕，驚醒美人睡。

Unit 7 Exercise

野斑鳩，別啁啾，驚醒美人睡。

你多舌的鸚鵡，勿要老囉嗦，

若驚醒美人睡，不與你干休。

Rhyme-scheme: a a b b

作者簡介：

Robert Burns（羅伯‧伯恩斯）**(1759–1796)**

蘇格蘭著名詩人，享年僅三十七歲。從小生長於貧苦農家，農忙之餘，仍不忘忙
中偷閒，努力用功。沒上過大學，然刻苦向學，如莎士比亞一樣，是一個自學
成功的例子。

說明：

此即世界名曲蘇格蘭民謠《阿頓河》之原文。由 J. E. Spilman 作曲，蕭而化譯
詞。

意境：

阿頓河位於蘇格蘭高原西南，流經阿爾郡 (Ayrshire)，潔靜如鏡，風景極美。詩
人羅伯‧伯恩斯生長於斯，從小即與此河結下不解之緣。

阿頓河在詩中呈現歷歷如繪之景象。一位樸質秀麗的小姑娘，躺在河畔，無憂無
慮，已入夢鄉，詩情畫意，潔靜安詳。

XIII Words Review

1. apartment *n.* 公寓
2. create *v.* 創造
3. custom *n.* 風俗
4. else *adv.* 其他
5. exciting *adj.* 令人興奮的
6. familiar *adj.* 熟悉的
7. feeling *n.* 感情；感覺
8. figure *v., n.* 估計；數字
9. final *adj.* 最後的
10. hate *v.* 恨
11. hobby *n.* 嗜好
12. illness *n.* 生病
13. imagine *v.* 想像
14. language *n.* 語言
15. long-term *adj.* 長程的；長期的
16. lucky *adj.* 幸運的
17. maybe *adv.* 可能
18. miss *v.* 想念；錯過
19. mistake *n.* 錯誤
20. nothing *n.* 沒有
21. perhaps *adv.* 或許
22. problem *n.* 問題
23. produce *v.* 生產
24. protect *v.* 保護
25. public *adj.* 大眾的；公共的
26. reason *n.* 理由
27. result *n.* 結果
28. role *n.* 角色
29. seem *v.* 似乎
30. sense *n.* 感官；感覺
31. service *n.* 服務
32. similar *adj.* 相似的
33. simple *adj.* 簡單的
34. smell *v.* 聞起來
35. solve *v.* 解決
36. sound *v.* 聽起來
37. stay *v.* 停留
38. successful *adj.* 成功的
39. surprise *n.* 驚訝，驚奇
40. system *n.* 系統；制度
41. unfamiliar *adj.* 不熟悉的
42. unpleasant *adj.* 令人不愉快的
43. wear *v.* 穿；磨
44. wonderful *adj.* 美妙的

8 Unit Eight

William Shakespeare

1. Who is William Shakespeare?
2. Do you know any stories written by William Shakespeare?
3. Do you know the story "Romeo and Juliet"?
   Do you know who wrote it? What is the story about?

William *Shakespeare* is the most famous playwright[1] of all time. He lived in England four hundred years ago and wrote *a series of* plays that have continuously[2] been performed[3] until this day. Shakespeare's plays have been so influential[4] that they have shaped the English language. His plays are about love, war, greed[5], jealousy[6] and almost every other human emotion. These are themes[7] that everyone can understand and this is why his plays have stayed popular[8] and become famous worldwide.

Shakespeare was born in 1564 in the old English market town of Stratford-upon-Avon. When he was eighteen, Shakespeare *got married to* a woman from his home town called Anne Hathaway. As a young man Shakespeare was fascinated by theatre[9], which at that time was the most popular form of entertainment[10]. In 1591 Shakespeare decided to fulfill[11] his ambition[12] and work in theatre. He therefore left his family and went to London, where he joined a theater company as an actor[13]. Once he settled[14] in London he began writing new plays for his actor friends to perform. After a few years he became well known in London as a talented[15] actor and playwright.

---

1. playwright [ˈpleˌraɪt]
2. continuously [kənˈtɪnjʊəslɪ]
3. perform [pɚˈfɔrm]
4. influential [ˌɪnflʊˈɛnʃəl]
5. greed [grid]
6. jealousy [ˈdʒɛləsɪ]
7. theme [θim]
8. popular [ˈpɑpjələ˞]
9. theatre [ˈθiətə˞]
10. entertainment [ˌɛntɚˈtenmənt]
11. fulfill [fʊlˈfɪl]
12. ambition [æmˈbɪʃən]
13. actor [ˈæktə˞]
14. settle [ˈsɛtl̩]
15. talented [ˈtæləntɪd]

Between 1591 and 1611 Shakespeare wrote thirty-seven 20
plays. Some of his most famous plays are: '*Romeo and Juliet,*'
'*Hamlet,*' '*Macbeth*' and '*King Lear.*' Shakespeare's greatest talent
was for writing the words of kings and rich people *as well as* for
writing the words of thieves[16] and poor people. Shakespeare's
writing was poetic[17] and beautiful and his plays were dramatic[18] 25
and often very sad. Many phrases[19] from his plays have passed
into the language and today are used by millions of people. For
example, people often say "the King's English," "fair play," and "to
catch cold." Some of Shakespeare's often quoted[20] lines are:

"To be or not to be, that is the question." (*Hamlet*) 30

"The course[21] of true love never did run smooth." (*A
Midsummer Night's Dream*)

"All the world's a stage,

And all the men and women merely[22] players." (*As You Like It*)

"What is in a name?" (*Romeo and Juliet*) 35

Many people believe '*Romeo and Juliet*' is the greatest love
story ever written. It is the story of two young people who *fall in
love* against the wishes of their families. Surrounded[23] by
violence[24], the love between Romeo and Juliet stays pure[25] until

---

16. thief [θif]
17. poetic [po'ɛtɪk]
18. dramatic [drə'mætɪk]
19. phrase [frez]
20. quote [kwot]
21. course [kors]
22. merely ['mɪrlɪ]
23. surround [sə'raʊnd]
24. violence ['vaɪələns]
25. pure [pjʊr]

40　the sad end of their own lives. ‘*Romeo and Juliet*’ has been performed by theatre companies around the world and even made into a Hollywood Movie. Today in the English language it is common to hear a youthful[26] lover called a "Young Romeo."

In his later years Shakespeare retired[27] to Stratford-upon-

45　Avon, where he died in 1616. *Ever since*, the house in which Shakespeare was born and the place where he was buried[28] have been kept as memorials[29]. Each year thousands of tourists come to Stratford-upon-Avon to visit these memorials and *pay* respect[30] *to* the greatest English writer that ever lived.

Vocabulary

1. playwright [ˈpleˌraɪt] *n.* C a writer of plays 劇作家
   William Shakespeare is a famous *playwright*.
2. continuously [kənˈtɪnjuəslɪ] *adv.* 連續不斷地
   John has been working for the theatre *continuously*.
3. perform [pɚˈfɔrm] *vi., vt.* to act or show especially in the presence of the public 表演
   The team will *perform* at the theatre weekly.
4. influential [ˌɪnfluˈɛnʃəl] *adj.* having great influence 有影響的
   The teaching of Confucius has been *influential*.
5. greed [grid] *n.* U a strong desire to have a lot of something, especially

26. youthful [ˈjuθfəl]　　28. bury [ˈbɛrɪ]　　30. respect [rɪˈspɛkt]
27. retire [rɪˈtaɪr]　　　29. memorial [məˈmorɪəl]

food, money or power 貪心；貪婪

Greed is the root of all evils.

6. jealousy [ˈdʒɛləsɪ] *n.* [C][U] (a) jealous feeling 嫉妒

His *jealousy* has caused the trouble.

7. theme [θim] *n.* [C] the subject of a talk, piece of writing, etc. 主題

The *theme* of the play is love.

8. popular [ˈpɑpjələ] *adj.* liked by many people 受歡迎的

The movie is very *popular* here.

9. theatre, theater [ˈθiətə] *n.* [C] a special place or building for the performance of plays 劇院

This is the biggest *theatre* in France.

10. entertainment [ˌɛntəˈtenmənt] *n.* [U] the act or profession of entertaining 娛樂

Watching television is a good form of *entertainment*.

11. fulfill [fʊlˈfil] *vt.* to carry out 完成；實現

Robert *fulfilled* his promise.

12. ambition [æmˈbɪʃən] *n.* [C][U] strong desire, especially over a long period, for success, power, wealth, etc. 雄心；野心

His *ambition* is to become a lawyer.

13. actor [ˈæktə] *n.* [C] a person who acts in a play or a film or on television 演員

Bill has become a popular *actor*.

14. settle [ˈsɛtl] *vi., vt.* to go and live in a place 定居

The Browns moved to the west and *settled* down there.

15. talented [ˈtæləntɪd] *adj.* having or showing talent 有才能的

Beethoven is a *talented* musician.

talent *n.*

Bach showed a great *talent* for music.

16. thief [θif] *n.* C a person who steals, especially without using violence
小偷

17. poetic [po'ɛtɪk] *adj.* of or like poets or poetry　有詩意的
The scenery is very *poetic*.

18. dramatic [drə'mætɪk] *adj.* exciting and unusual, like something that could
happen in a drama　戲劇性的
The plot of the story is very *dramatic*.

19. phrase [frez] *n.* C (in grammar) a group of words without a finite verb,
especially when they are used to form part of a sentence　片語
They like to use *phrases* of common people.

20. quote [kwot] *vi., vt.* to repeat in speech or writing the words of (a person, a
book, etc.)　引述
In his writing, Dan loved to *quote* old sayings.

21. course [kors] *n.* U the path along which something moves　進行

22. merely ['mɪrlɪ] *adv.* simply　僅僅；不過是…

23. surround [sə'raʊnd] *vt.* to be all around on every side　環繞；圍繞
The movie star is *surrounded* by his fans.

24. violence ['vaɪələns] *n.* U extreme force in action or feeling, especially
that causes damage, unrest, etc.　暴力
Violence can't solve problems.

25. pure [pjʊr] *adj.* not mixed with anything else　純潔的
The air is *pure* in the countryside.

26. youthful ['juθfəl] *adj.* young　年輕的
It is important to keep a *youthful* heart.

27. retire [rɪ'taɪr] *vi., vt.* to stop working at one's job, usually because of age
退休

The soldier *retired* at the age of 55.

28. bury [ˈbɛrɪ] *vt.* to put (a dead body) into a grave 埋葬

    The poet was *buried* in the graveyard.

29. memorial [məˈmorɪəl] *n.* C something, especially a stone monument, in memory of a person, event, etc. 紀念物

    We visited the CKS *Memorial* last Sunday.

    memorial *adj.*

    This is a *memorial* hospital for Dr. Mackay.

30. respect [rɪˈspɛkt] *n.* U 尊敬

    We show *respect* to our national heroes.

Idioms and Phrases

1. William Shakespeare 莎士比亞 (1564–1616)，英國詩人，劇作家

2. a series of... 一系列的…

   He wrote *a series of* books on love.

3. get married to... 與…結婚

   Bob *got married to* Amy last week.

4. as well as... 以及…

   The good news is for men *as well as* for women.

5. fall in love 戀愛

   Romeo *fell in love* with Juliet.

6. ever since 從那時起

   He came here for a holiday one month ago and he's lived here *ever since*.

   Ever since last year, Carl has been writing books.

7. pay respect to... 尊敬…

   We should *pay respect to* our teachers.

Exercise

I True or False

(　　) 1. William Shakespeare is the most famous playwright of all time.

(　　) 2. Shakespeare lived in England eight hundred years ago.

(　　) 3. His plays are about love, war, greed, and jealousy.

(　　) 4. Shakespeare was born in 1564 in Italy.

(　　) 5. When he was twenty, he was married to a woman.

(　　) 6. In 1591 Shakespeare decided to work in theatre.

(　　) 7. Between 1591 and 1611 Shakespeare wrote thirty-seven plays.

(　　) 8. One of his most famous plays is '*War and Peace*.'

(　　) 9. Shakespeare's writing was poetic and beautiful.

(　　) 10. Many people believe '*Romeo and Juliet*' is the greatest story about war ever written.

II Reading Comprehension

1. When and where was Shakespeare born?

2. How influential have Shakespeare's plays been?

3. What are Shakespeare's plays about?

4. How many plays did Shakespeare write between 1591 and 1611?

5. What is the greatest love story ever written?

6. In his later years where did Shakespeare retire to? When did he die?

7. Why do thousands of tourists come to Stratford-upon-Avon each year?

III Discussion

1. Who is the greatest playwright in your country?

2. Why is Shakespeare the most famous playwright of all time?

3. What are some of Shakespeare's plays?

4. Do you like Shakespeare's plays? Why or why not?

IV Vocabulary Selection

(　) 1. William Shakespeare is a famous _____.

    (A) playwright　(B) dancer　(C) singer

(　) 2. Shakespeare wrote a _____ of plays.

    (A) series　(B) little　(C) many

(　) 3. Good exercise has kept me in good _____.

    (A) play　(B) shape　(C) greed

(　) 4. Music is an international _____.

    (A) story　(B) jealousy　(C) language

(　) 5. _____ is the root of all evils.

    (A) Form　(B) Greed　(C) Market

(　) 6. Many tourists were _____ by the great scenery.

    (A) fascinated　(B) married　(C) decided

(　) 7. The lawyer tried to _____ the problem for us.

    (A) join　(B) phrase　(C) settle

(　) 8. The little girl is a _____ famous musician.

    (A) quoted　(B) talented　(C) retired

(　) 9. The child tried to _____ his own ambition.

    (A) fulfill　(B) respect　(C) perform

（　）10. My favorite _____ is seeing movies.

      (A) decision   (B) violence   (C) entertainment

V Word Forms

Verb	Noun	Adjective
perform	performance	performing
–	greed	greedy
humanize	humanity	human
popularize	popularity	popular
emotionalize	emotion	emotional
–	ambition	ambitious
fulfill	fulfillment	–
–	violence	violent
–	talent	talented
dramatize	drama	dramatic
respect	respect	respectful（尊敬的）
		respectable（可敬的）
		respective（個別的）

1. The circus is having a _____ (perform) now.

2. The _____ (greed) sailor tried to kill the others.

3. Advances in science help all _____ (human).

4. The _____ (popular) of the singer is very great.

5. The movie actors are very _____ (emotion).

6. Napolean was a very _____ (ambition) emperor.

7. The clerk's _____ (fulfill) of duties deserves praise.

8. No _____ (violent) is allowed in the meeting.

9. Thomas Edison is a very _____ (talent) scientist.

10. His hard life of learning is very _____ (drama).

11. We should be _____ (respect) to our teachers.

VI Idioms and Phrases

(*Make any change in verb forms, if necessary.*)

as well as	some of	millions of	fall in love
around the world	ever since	pay respect to	

1. Judy _____ her classmates will join the party.

2. The old soldier came here to _____ his teacher.

3. The musician is taking a trip _____.

4. _____ my good friends will take me home.

5. _____ the singer arrived at the show, he has started singing.

6. Every year _____ tourists go abroad for sightseeing.

7. Kitty said: "I have _____ with you."

VII Matching

_____ 1. Shakespeare was born   a. and went to London.

_____ 2. He therefore left his family b. against the wishes of their families.

_____ 3. These are themes   c. known in London as a playwright.

_____ 4. They fell in love   d. that everyone can understand.

_____ 5. Ever since, the house   e. in 1564 in England.

_____ 6. He became well   f. has been kept as memorials.

VIII Cloze Test

Ever since, the house ____1____ which Shakespeare ____2____ born and the place ____3____ he was ____4____ have been ____5____ as memorials. Each year thousands ____6____ tourists come ____7____ Stratford-upon-Avon to ____8____ these ____9____ and pay ____10____ to the greatest English writer that ever lived.

(   ) 1. (A) in   (B) of   (C) on   (D) to

(   ) 2. (A) is   (B) was   (C) were   (D) are

(   ) 3. (A) what   (B) that   (C) which   (D) where

(   ) 4. (A) quoted   (B) visited   (C) called   (D) buried

(   ) 5. (A) joined   (B) settled   (C) kept   (D) made

(   ) 6. (A) in   (B) of   (C) from   (D) to

(   ) 7. (A) off   (B) in   (C) to   (D) from

(   ) 8. (A) fulfill   (B) visit   (C) surround   (D) perform

(   ) 9. (A) memorials   (B) markets   (C) emotions   (D) themes

(   ) 10. (A) form   (B) phrase   (C) respect   (D) ambition

IX Translation

1. 威廉・莎士比亞是有史以來最著名的劇作家。他於四百年前住在英國,並寫了一系列的戲劇,到目前為止仍持續在上演。

   William Shakespeare is the most _____ playwright of _____ time. He lived _____ England four _____ years ago and wrote a _____ of plays that have _____ been _____ until _____ day.

2. 他一在倫敦定居之後,便開始寫作新的劇本讓他的演員朋友去演出。幾年後，他在倫敦成名為具有才氣的演員及劇作家。

Once he _____ in London he began _____ new plays for his actor _____ to _____ . After a _____ years he became well _____ in London _____ a _____ actor and _____ .

X Grammar

Adverb 副詞 (Adv.)

*定義：副詞為用來修飾動詞、形容詞、副詞及整個句子的字。通常字尾為 "ly"。

*種類：副詞可分類如下：

簡單副詞	nicely, happily, well, soon, very, etc.
疑問副詞	when, where, what, why, how, which, etc.
關係副詞	when, where, how, why, etc.

Focus 8.1.1

請在 A, B, C, D 中選出一個最符合題句的正確答案。

(　　) He discussed the subject _____ .

    (A) fullest　　(B) complete　　(C) deeply　　(D) fastly

〈解析〉1. 副詞的形態大部分皆有 "ly"。

      2. 副詞修飾動詞、形容詞、副詞及整個句子。在本句，副詞 "deeply" 修飾動詞 "discussed"。

〈Ans〉C

Unit 8 Exercise

Focus 8.1.2

請在 A, B, C, D 中選出一個最符合題句的正確答案。

( ) Shakespeare's plays have _____ been performed until this day.

(A) continued　(B) continuous　(C) continuously　(D) continuing

〈解析〉1. 副詞修飾動詞。

2. 本句 "continuously"（繼續地）修飾 "performed"（表演）。

〈Ans〉C

Focus 8.1.3

請在 A, B, C, D 中選出一個最符合題句的正確答案。

( ) Shakespeare became _____ known in London as a talented playwright.

(A) fair　(B) well　(C) good　(D) people

〈解析〉1. "known" 為 "know" 的過去分詞作形容詞用，修飾它的字必須為副詞。

2. 只有 "well" 為副詞。

〈Ans〉B

Focus 8.2.1

請在 A, B, C, D 中找出一個不符合正確語法的錯誤之處。

( ) At first the significant popular songs of the United States were
　　　　　　　　(A)　　　　(B)　　　　　　　　　　　　　　(C)
politic motivated.
　(D)

〈解析〉副詞修飾動詞、形容詞、副詞及整個句子。

e.g. He is actively motivated.

"motivated" 為動詞 "motivate" 的過去分詞，所以要修飾它，必須為副詞。

〈Ans〉D, politic → politically

Focus 8.2.2

請在 A, B, C, D 中找出一個不符合正確語法的錯誤之處。

( ) <u>Some of</u> Shakespeare's <u>common</u> quoted <u>lines</u> <u>are</u> here.
　　　(A)　　　　　　　　(B)　　　　　　(C)　(D)

〈解析〉副詞才可修飾動詞的過去分詞。

e.g. Shakespeare is widely respected.

要修飾動詞 "quote" 的過去分詞 "quoted" 就必須用副詞。

〈Ans〉B, common → commonly

Focus 8.2.3

請在 A, B, C, D 中找出一個不符合正確語法的錯誤之處。

( ) <u>Shakespeare's plays</u> are <u>well extremely</u> <u>presented</u> at this <u>theatre</u>.
　　　(A)　　　　　　　　(B)　　　　(C)　　　　　(D)

〈解析〉副詞修飾動詞，另一副詞再修飾此副詞。

次序：大小強度副詞＋性質副詞＋動詞

e.g. He is very much tired.

He is very well known.

The news is much widely spread.

"extremely" 修飾 "well"，"well" 再修飾 "presented"。

〈Ans〉B, well extremely → extremely well

Unit 8 Exercise

XI Short Story

Helen Keller

Helen Keller was born in Alabama in 1880. When she was twenty months old, she got an illness. After her illness Helen could not hear or see. She was deaf and blind. Helen was a difficult child. Her parents did not know what to do.

Finally, when Helen was seven years old, her parents got her a special teacher. Her name was Miss Anne Sullivan. Miss Sullivan worked with Helen all day. She took Helen's hand and spelled a word in her hand. Helen soon learned to say what she wanted in this way.

In 1900 Helen entered Radcliffe College. Miss Sullivan sat next to Helen in class. She spelled all the words into Helen's hand. Miss Sullivan also read to Helen all the time. At that time there were only a few books for the blind. These were Braille books. They had a special alphabet made with dots that blind people could read with their fingers. Helen graduated from Radcliffe with honors, or very high grades.

Helen wrote books like *The Story of My Life* and *Midstream—My Later Life*. She also wrote magazine articles and spoke all over the country. She learned to speak. It was not easy to understand her. Miss Sullivan repeated what Helen said. Helen spoke about the deaf and blind. People everywhere became interested. There was new hope for the deaf and blind.

XII Poem

Sonnet 116

—William Shakespeare

Let me not to the marriage of true minds

Admit impediments. Love is not love

Which alters when it alteration finds,

Or bends with the remover to remove.

O, no, it is an ever-fixed mark

That looks on tempests and is never shaken;

It is the star to every wand'ring bark,

Whose worth's unknown, although his height be taken.

Love's not Time's fool, though rosy lips and cheeks

Within his bending sickle's compass come;

Love alters not with his brief hours and weeks,

But bears it out even to the edge of doom.

If this be error and upon me proved,

I never writ, nor no man ever loved.

第一一六首十四行詩

「韶光易逝愛不渝」

——威廉‧莎士比亞

兩真心結合　我得承認

不容阻擾。　愛不算真愛

如發現對方變心　也跟著變心

或看見情況改變　便棄舊迎新。

Unit 8 Exercise

啊，不，愛是永遠堅定的燈塔

面臨暴風雨　永不動搖；

愛是北極星　指引一切迷途船隻，

雖高度可測　但價值無限。

愛不是時間的玩物，雖然朱唇粉頰

遲早總不免被無情歲月之彎刀刈除；

愛不跟隨短促韶光起變化，

就到世界末日邊緣　永遠不渝。

如這話有誤　確不足置信，

那麼算我沒寫過詩，沒人有過愛情。

Rhyme-scheme: a b a b c d c d e f e f g g

作者簡介：

William Shakespeare（莎士比亞）**(1564–1616)**

生於英格蘭中部的史特拉福鎮。小時候曾上過文法學校，相當於國民小學，後因
父親經商失敗，被迫輟學，自力謀生。十九歲時，與比他大七歲的安娜‧哈莎薇
結婚。因自幼就對戲劇發生興趣，一五八六年他獨自前往倫敦尋求戲劇上的發
展。他勤苦好學，抱著沉默、努力的心情，靜觀千變萬化的社會環境並吸收新
知，他的創造力因而增加。

他在倫敦的劇團裡當一名演員，演了十八年。平日利用閒暇寫作，陸續出版，慢
慢獲得名氣。主要創作分兩方面：戲劇與詩。戲劇名著到目前仍為各界所研究與
表演。英詩尤以非常綺麗動人的《十四行詩》(Sonnet) 著名於世。

說明：

第一一六首十四行詩

「韶光易逝愛不渝」

莎士比亞的《第一一六首十四行詩‧韶光易逝愛不渝》是一首著名的充滿愛情的情詩。古今中外，無數的男男女女因讀了這首動人的名詩而深受感動，許願終生，留下美好的愛情故事與回憶。

XIII Words Review

1. beautiful *adj.* 美麗的
2. bear *v.* 出生
   bear bore born
3. common *adj.* 普遍的
4. company *n.* 公司
5. England *n.* 英國
6. form *n.* 形式
7. human *adj.* 人類的
8. join *v.* 參加
9. once *conj.* 一旦
10. play *n.* 戲劇
11. stay *v.* 仍然是；停留
12. tourist *n.* 觀光客

Index I

Index II

超級科學家系列
SUPER SCIENTISTS

中英對照，既可學英語又可了解偉人小故事哦！

當彗星掠過哈雷眼前，
當蘋果落在牛頓頭頂，
當電燈泡在愛迪生手中亮起……
一個個求知的心靈與真理所碰撞出的火花，
那就是《超級科學家系列》！

神祕元素：居禮夫人的故事　含CD190元

望遠天際：伽利略的故事　含CD190元

爆炸性的發現：諾貝爾的故事　含CD190元

宇宙教授：愛因斯坦的故事　含CD190元

電燈的發明：愛迪生的故事　含CD190元

光的顏色：牛頓的故事　定價160元

蠶寶寶的祕密：巴斯德的故事　含CD190元

命運的彗星：哈雷的故事　含CD190元

一本最符合英語學習者需求的辭典！

三民 全球英漢辭典

莊信正、楊榮華主編

◎ 詞彙蒐羅詳盡，全書詞目超過93,000項。

◎ 釋義清晰明瞭，以樹枝狀的概念，將每個字彙分成「基本義」與「衍生義」，使讀者對字彙的理解更具整體概念。

◎ 以學習者的需要為出發點，將臺灣英語學習者最需要的語言資料詳實涵括在本書各項單元中。

◎ 新增「搭配用詞」一欄，列出詞語間的常用組合，增進你的語感，幫助你寫出、說出道地的英文。

讓你掌握英語的慣用搭配方式，學會道道地地的英語！

三民 新英漢辭典（增訂完美版）

◎ 收錄詞目增至67,500項（詞條增至46,000項）。

◎ 新增「搭配」欄，列出常用詞語間的組合關係，讓你掌握英語的慣用搭配，說出道地的英語。

◎ 附有精美插圖千餘幅，輔助詞義理解。

◎ 附錄包括詳盡的「英文文法總整理」、「發音要領解說」，提升學習效率。

一般辭典查不到的文化意涵，讓它來告訴你！

美國日常語辭典

◎ 描寫美國真實面貌，讓你不只學好美語，更進一步瞭解美國社會與文化！

◎ 廣泛蒐集美國人日常生活的語彙，是一本能伴你暢遊美國的最佳工具書！

◎ 從日常生活的角度出發，自日常用品、飲食文化、文學、藝術、到常見俚語，帶領你感受美語及其所代表的文化內涵，讓學習美語的過程不再只是背誦單字和強記文法句型的單調練習。

專為需要經常查閱最新詞彙的你設計！

三民 袖珍英漢辭典

◎收錄詞條高達58,000字，從最新的專業術語、時事用詞到日常生活所需詞彙全數網羅！

◎輕巧便利的口袋型設計，最適於外出攜帶！